Praise for *Leaving Paradise*

"Elkeles writes convincingly about family tensions, retreating from painful reality, and teens outgrowing their old skins."

—*School Library Journal*

return
to
paradise

SIMONE ELKELES

return to paradise

flux

Woodbury, Minnesota

First Edition
First Printing, 2010

Book design by Steffani Sawyer
Cover design by Lisa Novak
Cover image © Image Source/PunchStock

Flux, an imprint of Llewellyn Worldwide Ltd.

This is a work of fiction. Names, characters, places, and incidents are either the product of the author's imagination or are used fictitiously, and any resemblance to actual persons, living or dead, business establishments, events, or locales is entirely coincidental. Cover models used for illustrative purposes only and may not endorse or represent the book's subject.

Library of Congress Cataloging-in-Publication Data
Elkeles, Simone.
  Return to Paradise / Simone Elkeles.—1st ed.
    p. cm.
  Sequel to: Leaving Paradise.
  Summary: In alternating chapters, Caleb and Maggie relate the struggles of being reunited after nearly a year apart when both join a group of teens affected by drunk driving, and finally facing their true feelings for one another.
  ISBN 978-0-7387-1868-2
  [1. Interpersonal relations—Fiction. 2. People with disabilities—Fiction. 3. Drunk driving—Fiction. 4. Secrets—Fiction.]
  I. Title.
  PZ7.E42578Ret 2010
  [Fic]—dc22
                                        2010017235

Flux
Llewellyn Worldwide Ltd.
2143 Wooddale Drive
Woodbury, MN 55125-2989
www.fluxnow.com

Printed in the United States of America

For
Erika Danou-Hasan,
Ruth Kaufman,
and Marilyn Brant—
three women who continue to remind me that
friendship is selfless and has no boundaries.

Acknowledgments

I want to thank Brian Farrey, Steven Pomije, Sandy Sullivan, Marissa Pederson, and all the Flux staff for helping me work on this book and for letting me continue Maggie and Caleb's story. You've made my fans beyond happy.

My agent Kristin Nelson has been a rock, and her support overwhelms me. Thanks for being my champion. It means the world to me!

My extreme thanks, as always, to Karen Harris for her support and friendship … without you my books wouldn't make sense to anyone but myself. I wouldn't have been sane this year without my amazing assistant Melissa Hermann—thank you for your hard work and dedication a million times over! And to Rob Adelman, the guy who brings the word *amazing* to the next level.

I can't thank Samantha, Brett, Fran, and Moshe enough for letting me write my books and neglect the laundry and dishes. I'll make up for it … one day. Or not (don't tell them my little secret … I hate doing laundry and dishes!).

Last but not least, thank you to my passionate and incredible fans … they are my inspiration for writing books and mean more to me than I can put into words.

ONE

Caleb

Some people are damn lucky. Unfortunately I've never been one of those people. In fact, I think I'm one of those guys destined to always be caught in the crossfire. As I sit in the back of a squad car with handcuffs digging into my wrists, I think back to the first time I got arrested, almost two years ago.

I'd been drinking.

I was wasted.

And I was arrested for a crime I didn't commit.

Didn't matter, though. I got locked in juvie for a year anyway, mostly because I pled guilty to the hit-and-run drunk driving charges.

This time I'm getting arrested for drugs. Except I didn't

smoke, inhale, ingest, snort, shoot up, or buy the shit. Okay, I admit I was living in a drug house. It was either keep a roof over my head and ignore the illegal stuff going on around me, or live on the streets.

I chose the roof. Looking back, maybe it wasn't the wisest choice. Living on the streets sounds mighty tempting right now. Nothing is worse than being locked up like a caged animal and relinquishing control of your own life. Being told when to shit, shower, shave, eat, and sleep isn't my idea of paradise. But then again, Paradise, where I grew up, wasn't paradise either. I'm wondering if paradise is just some word in the dictionary with the definition: *this doesn't fucking exist.*

I lean my head against the back seat of the squad car, wondering how I'm gonna get out of this. I have no money, no real friends, and my family ... well, I haven't had any contact with them since I left Paradise eight months ago.

When we arrive at the police station, the cop escorts me to a lady who has the exciting job of taking my mug shot. Then the cop orders me to his desk and introduces himself as Lieutenant Ramsey.

"Don't try anything stupid," he tells me as he unlocks the handcuff on my right wrist and secures it to a metal hook on his desk so if I wanted to flee I'd have to lug a fifty-pound desk with me. Needless to say, I'm not going anywhere.

After asking me a bunch of questions, he leaves me alone. I look around for Rio, one of my five roommates.

We all got busted at the same time, when Rio and another one of our roommates were selling a crapload of meth to three guys who, if you ask me, looked like undercover cops who were just dressed up as badass gangsters. I think it was the gold tooth on one of the guys that gave it away. It looked like it'd been glued on and I could have sworn it became loose at one point and he swallowed it.

That was right before they pulled out their guns and yelled for us to kneel on the ground and put our hands on our heads. I'd been watching some reality show about a pawn shop, because the last thing I needed was to be involved in Rio's business.

Rio had asked me to help him make some runs a couple times, and I did. But I don't get off on selling drugs to guys who're so desperate to get high they'll give me their last dime to get it. The last time I was supposed to sell drugs for Rio, it was to a guy with three kids. He brought his three kids to our house, and when I saw their long, drawn faces and their ragged, torn clothes, I couldn't do it. I refused to sell him the stuff. Not that that makes me a good person or anything, especially because I know if I didn't sell it to him someone else would.

"Listen, Caleb," Ramsey says as he opens up a file folder with my name on the tab at the top. "You've got yourself in big trouble. Chicago judges aren't lenient on repeaters, especially when they're living in drug houses with over fifty thousand worth of meth and Z-tabs."

"I'm not a dealer," I tell him. "I work at Chicago Recycling."

"Just because you've got a job doesn't mean you don't deal." He picks up his phone and hands me the receiver. "You get one phone call. Tell me what number to dial."

I put the receiver down on his desk. "I waive my right to a call."

"Family? Friends?" he suggests.

I shake my head. "Don't got any."

Ramsey rests the handset back on the phone. "Don't you want someone to bail you out? The judge'll set bail later today or tomorrow. You should be prepared."

When I don't respond, he flips through my file. He looks up after a couple of minutes. "It says here Damon Manning was your transition counselor."

Damon Manning was supposed to make sure I stayed out of trouble back when I got released from juvie. He was a big black guy who scared my mom to death when he walked in our house during his scheduled visits. Damon assigned me my community service job and constantly drilled me on how to transition from being in jail to being back at home. He wouldn't take one-word responses or silence for an answer. The guy was a hardass who didn't take shit from anyone, and whenever I fucked up he let me know I better shape up or he would be personally responsible for telling the judge to lock me back up. I had no doubt that he'd do it, too.

Ramsey jots a number down and sets it in front of me.

"What's this?"

"Damon Manning's phone number."

"And why would I want it?" I ask him.

"If you don't have family or friends to bail you out, I suggest you call him."

I shake my head and say, "No way."

Ramsey pushes the phone toward me and leans back in his chair. "Call him. If you don't, I will."

"Why?"

"Because I read Damon's reports on you, and he's rarely wrong about his assessments."

"What did he write?" That I was a complete fuckup who deserved to be locked up permanently?

"Why don't you call him and ask him yourself? You're in big trouble, Caleb. You need someone on your side right now."

I look at the phone and shake my head in frustration. Ramsey doesn't look like he's giving me a choice. I pick up the phone and dial the number.

"This is Damon," a deep voice answers.

I clear my throat. "Umm...this is Caleb. Caleb Becker."

"Why are you callin' me?"

"I kind of got in trouble," I say, then clear my throat. I take a deep breath and reluctantly blurt out, "I need your help."

"Help? I didn't know you knew that word."

I briefly explain the situation. He sighs heavily a bunch of times, but says he's on his way over to the station. After my call, I'm escorted to a holding cell and wait for him. An hour later I'm told I have a visitor and am led to what I assume is one of the interrogation rooms. Oh, man. If things weren't bad enough, I have a feeling they're about to get worse as a very pissed-off Damon walks through the metal bulletproof door.

"What the hell did you get yourself into, Becker?"

"A shitload of trouble," I tell him.

Damon crosses his arms on his chest. "I could have sworn you were a guy who made one mistake and was going to turn his life around." He gets a distant, almost sad look on his face, but it's quickly masked. "I got to admit you reminded me of myself when I was your age."

"Yeah, well, you were obviously wrong."

He narrows his eyes at me. "Was I?"

This isn't the way it was supposed to be. I left Paradise to make everything better, but all I've managed to do is fuck things up for myself. I look Damon straight in the eye. "I didn't do it," I tell him. "I'm not a dealer."

"Why should I believe you?"

"Because it's the truth." I let out a breath, knowing it's a lost cause to plead my case but doing it anyway. "I don't expect you to believe me."

"Have you lied to me in the past?"

I nod.

"About what?"

I close my eyes and shake my head. I can't tell Damon that I wasn't the one who hit Maggie. I told Leah I'd take that secret to the grave. I can't betray my own twin. Not now, and not ever. "Forget it."

"You're on the wrong path," Damon tells me.

"I didn't have a choice." I let out a long, slow breath and decide to level with him. About some stuff, anyway. "I found out my mom was addicted to meds. I think me being home made it worse. She kept expecting me to fake it that everything was okay. My entire family went along with the bullshit. I couldn't. Maggie was the only one keeping me sane, but I couldn't see her without getting shit from the cops, my parents, her mom, and even you. You once said I should get out of Paradise instead of getting close to Maggie. So now I'm here."

"Living with a drug dealer isn't a better option," Damon says, stating the obvious.

"It was a roof over my head."

"There are always options other than living with thugs," Damon tells me.

"Yeah, right." I look down at the red mark the handcuffs left on my skin. I seem to be all out of options right now.

"I'm really disappointed in you."

Disappointed is better than angry. I've seen Damon angry. He stiffens up like a bull with a thorn up his ass. Hell, when I got suspended from school for fighting, Damon looked ready to single-handedly kick my ass. The guy is huge and must weigh close to two-eighty. I'm not a lightweight, but he could sit on me and crush my bones.

"I'll be right back," Damon says, then leaves me alone in the room.

Ramsey comes back a half hour later, with Damon following in his wake. The officer sits on the edge of the small table in the room and looks down at me. "You're lucky, kid."

I'm about to be tossed in jail. I'm not feeling lucky right about now.

"I just talked to Judge Hanson," Damon says. "You'll have your arraignment this afternoon, and I'll pay any bail set. I'm friends with the district attorney who'll help you."

"Why would you do that for me?" I ask.

"Because someone did it for me a while back. There's one condition," he says.

Here it comes. The ax is about to fall. "What?"

My ex–transition counselor has a stern look on his face. "You join Re-START."

"What's that?"

"It's a group of kids whose lives have been affected by reckless teen driving. We're traveling for a month together, and each participant shares their story with various groups of kids in the Midwest. We'll be roughing it, so don't expect fancy hotels or the royal treatment. We'll be staying in dorms and campgrounds. This arrest isn't about drugs, Caleb. It's a direct result of your accident in Paradise. Join the program and help others. If you don't agree to come with me, I'm out of here. If I leave, I have no doubt they'll lock you up for good and throw away the key. You're eighteen now. If you thought juvie was awful, I guarantee that adult lockup will be one hundred times worse."

"So I really don't have a choice?"

"You do. Stay here and enjoy the fine hospitality of our state prisons, or get off your ass and follow me."

So there isn't a choice. One of the options is something I'd do practically anything to avoid. Even if it includes spending time with my old transition counselor.

We don't speak much the entire one-and-a-half-hour drive out to Redwood. He tries to ask me questions and I do my best to dodge them. When we pull up the driveway of a one-story duplex, he explains, "You'll sleep at my place tonight, and meet up with the rest of the group tomorrow afternoon."

Inside, I drop my duffle next to a faded plaid couch. On the mantle above the empty fireplace is a picture of Damon with a little boy, about eight years old, in a Little League uniform.

"Is he yours?" I ask him, wondering how this guy ended up living alone in a small town in the middle of the boondocks of Illinois. Paradise isn't too far away from here.

"Yeah."

It's obvious from the look of the place he lives alone. There's no artwork on the bare white walls. The place isn't like my house back in Paradise—it's too plain and too unused, like he just comes here to sleep and that's it.

"You divorced?" I ask.

"You gonna stop asking questions? I think I liked you better on the ride here, when you didn't talk at all."

After Damon makes a surprisingly good dinner of chicken and rice that reminds me of my mom's cooking, he heads down a narrow hall to bed. It's quiet in the house. I'm not used to this much silence. At Rio's place, there were always people partying or coming in and out at all hours. I didn't mind, because I don't sleep much anyway.

I turn the light off although I know I'm not going to get much sleep tonight. It'll be like usual ... every fifteen minutes I'll wake up and stare at the ceiling and pray for sleep to come. It does, but in such short spurts I wonder what it'd be like to get a full night's sleep with no interruptions. That hasn't happened for years ... since before the accident.

In the morning I'm eating some healthy whole-grain type of cereal when Damon walks into the kitchen. I can't help but ask, "Why did you help me?"

"Because I think you're a good kid," he says, his back to me as he stands in front of the stove and fries some eggs. "You just have to make better choices."

In the late afternoon, we throw our bags in the car. Damon stops off at the Redwood community center, where a big white van is waiting for us. He gets summoned into the building and tells me to hang by the van and introduce myself to the rest of the group. There's two other guys and three girls standing there waiting with their baggage.

When one of the girls moves aside and I get a glimpse of the person she was shielding, my entire body goes numb.

Maggie.

TWO

Maggie

I watch my protein bar fall onto the blacktop in slow motion, and the bite in my mouth tastes like dust. *What is Caleb doing here?* Where has he been the past eight months? He left town without a trace after our brief and crazy relationship. Why didn't he try to reach me, or at least give me a sign that he's alive?

He's got those same blue eyes, that same chiseled face, and those same lean muscles peeking out of his T-shirt. He's real, and live, and walking right toward me.

I can't look away, even though I desperately want to.

He lets out a slow breath and says, "This is kinda awkward, huh." His voice sounds familiar but different. It's got an edge to it that wasn't there the last time we saw each other.

"Yeah," I manage to squeak out. Umm...

"How've you been?"

I can't answer that question. It's too fake. If he cared how I've been, he would have figured out a way to see me or talk to me. He left me before Christmas, before New Year's, before Valentine's Day, before my birthday, before prom and graduation. Before I got the news I'd have a permanent limp for the rest of my life without any hope of a full recovery. "What are you doing here?"

He shrugs. "I was asking myself that same question this morning."

One of the other guys standing with us, the one with long curly hair that falls in his face, farts. What's worse is that he makes a big show of moaning and pushing it out, like a little kid.

"Dude, do you mind?" Caleb asks.

"What?" the guy says, unfazed. "I had to let it rip."

"Let it rip when you're alone, man. Don't be a fuckin' prick."

"What are you, the fart police?" the guy says, stepping toward Caleb. Caleb stands tall, as if he's been in a lot of fights and isn't afraid of adding another one to his tally.

This is unreal. I can't feel my toes because I'm in shock, and Caleb and this guy are going to get into a fight over... farting?

"Cool it, guys," bellows a rough voice. A tall black guy

with a clipboard points to me. "Maggie, can I have a word with you for a minute? In private." He points to Caleb. "You too, Becker. *Now.*"

I follow the guy away from the van, painfully aware that Caleb is following close behind. I'm tempted to turn around and demand to know where he's been, but I don't even know if I could get the words out.

The guy stops at a picnic table and drops his clipboard on it. He introduces himself to me as Damon Manning, the senior leader and chaperone of our group, then looks pained as he says, "Obviously, you two can't be on this trip together. Maggie, I had no idea my assistant put you in as the replacement after Heather dropped out."

"I'll drop out," Caleb offers eagerly.

"The hell you will, Becker. You've got no choice but to do this."

That means Damon expects me to drop out. If I was the old Maggie, the one who was afraid of the least bit of conflict or confrontation, I'd drop out in a heartbeat. But I'm stronger now, and I don't back down from anything. Even Caleb.

I turn to Damon with determination. "I'm not dropping out."

"Maggie, I'm sorry but it's not going to work with both of you—"

"I'm not leaving," I interrupt.

Damon rubs a hand over his bald head and sighs. I can tell he's wavering … at least a little bit. What can I say to convince him I don't have to quit the trip just because Caleb happens to be on it? Truth is, being with Caleb will be a challenge—a huge one I hadn't expected. But I decide I'm going to prove it to myself and to him that I've moved on. I don't let the past dictate my life anymore. We're both eighteen now, both considered adults in the eyes of the law.

"This is a bad idea," Damon chimes in. "A *really* bad idea."

"Can I talk to Caleb alone?" I ask him.

Damon looks from me to Caleb. "Okay. You've got five minutes."

When Damon walks away, I swallow hard and force myself to face Caleb. He looks worn out, but at the same time a fierce strength radiates from him.

I used to think he was everything I wanted and needed. If I had Caleb Becker at my side, my life would be okay. And it was, for a little while at least.

"It's been eight months," I say in a small voice. Thinking of how much I've missed him makes my eyes well up. I blink and pray my tears don't fall. Not now, when I have to stay strong. I say something, anything, so I don't lose it. "You missed graduation."

"I missed a lot of things," he says, then slowly starts to reach out his hand before he shoves both hands in his pockets.

I know I probably look pathetic. I *feel* pathetic. But I'm sick of feeling sorry for myself. I've had to move on.

I've gotten stronger every day. I can't get sucked back into the soap opera of Caleb's life. I won't let that happen.

I look at the big white van that's supposed to take us on a four-week trip together. We're going to share our stories publicly, hoping to prevent others from experiencing what happened to us. I bite my lip at the irony. How can we do that, when the truth of Caleb's and my accident is still buried?

I kick at some loose pebbles of tar on the blacktop. "He said you have no choice but to go on this trip. Why?"

Arms folded, Caleb leans against the picnic table and sighs. "Okay, here's the deal. Big surprise: I got myself in trouble again. It's either this program, or I go to jail. The ball's in your court, Maggie. You want me to quit, I will. I'll take the consequences."

The last thing I want is Caleb back in jail. I'm afraid to ask for details of how he got into trouble, so I don't. If he wants to tell me, he will. But I know he won't because he doesn't know how to trust anyone, least of all *me*. I might have been a part of his life once, but now I'm not. I'm a stranger to him, and he's a stranger to me.

"It's only four weeks," I tell him. "I think we can handle it."

"Four weeks stuck in a van together, and then you never have to see me again."

I close my eyes when he says that. He shouldn't disappear again. His sister needs him, and his mother struggles every day with her prescription drug addiction. "After the trip, you should go back to Paradise."

"Not gonna happen, so get that thought out of your head."

Forgetting my sadness and gathering courage, I stand up straight and look him in the eye. "You know what I think?"

"What?"

"I think the tough and stoic Caleb Becker takes the easy way out." There, I said it.

"My life is a lot of things, Maggie, but easy isn't one of them," he says. He clears his throat. "And if you think seeing you right now is a piece of cake for me, guess again..." His voice trails off.

"Maybe this was fate giving us a second chance at saying goodbye. You know, before we both go our separate ways again."

"That must be what it is," he says sarcastically. "So you're absolutely cool with going on this trip together?"

I clear my throat and look over at the van. "I'm cool with it as long as you are."

Pushing himself away from the table, he walks away from me and heads over to Damon. They talk for a second, then Caleb tosses his duffle in the back of the van and climbs inside.

"Caleb said you worked it out," Damon says to me when I limp over to the van.

"It's only four weeks. It'll be fine."

Damon looks about as convinced as I feel, but I assure him the past is behind us and we'll get beyond it. I really hope I'm not lying to myself.

In the van, the two girls who I met this morning are sitting in the front seat. The girl named Erin has a pierced nose and lip and has tattoos running up and down her bare arm. She's reading a book while leaning against the window. The other girl, Trish, has long, really shiny blonde hair and could definitely pass for one of the popular cheerleaders back in Paradise. She has dark makeup on her eyes and wears light pink lipstick. It looks good on her.

I purposely avoid even glancing at the rear bench—I'm not going to look where *he's* sitting—and slide next to Matt on the middle bench. I know Matt from physical therapy, since his appointments are usually after mine on Wednesday nights. Matt lost three quarters of his left arm, and his right arm is scarred, but I'm not sure exactly what happened. I'm sure I'll find out once we share our stories.

Matt gives me a friendly but reserved smile. "I didn't know you'd be here," he says.

"It was a last-minute thing," I tell him, eyeing Trish and Erin in the seat in front of us and wondering if Caleb will decide to ditch the trip at the very last second. Part of me wants him to leave, but the other part wants him to stay so I can prove to myself that I'm truly over him, that the pain that lingered after he left is gone.

My pulse quickens when I hear Caleb shifting in his seat behind us. It's not a good sign that I'm hyper-aware of his every movement. I'm probably in for four weeks of real torture—maybe even worse than the year of physical therapy after the accident.

Never mind how I felt when Caleb abandoned me. In the weeks and months after he left town, I prayed that he'd come back. I used to keep my light on at night, so if he came back he'd see it as a sign that I was waiting for him. He lived next door, so I would gaze out my window for hours on end, hoping to see the light on in his room. My fantasy was that he would tell me he made a huge mistake by leaving Paradise.

But he never did.

In the end, I realized I had relied on him too much.

Damon gets into the driver's seat and turns around. "Well, guys, this is it. Our first stop is a camp-based summer school for teens. We'll be sleeping in cabins at their campground tonight, and you'll be expected to share your stories with them. Tomorrow we'll leave and head to our second gig. But right now, take a second to introduce yourselves while we're waiting for Lenny. As y'all know, I'm Damon Manning and I'm your chaperone."

"I'm Trish," Trish says, with an edge to her voice that implies *don't talk to me unless I want you to.*

Erin doesn't look up from her book as she says in a small voice, "I'm Erin."

Matt clears his throat. "I'm Matt."

"I'm Maggie," I say, unable to resist a glance at Caleb.

He looks like he'd rather go diving in shark or piranha-infested waters than be in this van. He stares at the floor mat. "I'm Caleb."

"And I'm Lenny," the guy who passed gas says, practically bouncing into the van and slipping into the spot next to Caleb.

Caleb winces. "Dude, if you fart again I'm gonna kick your ass."

"Caleb, no threatening the other members of the group," Damon orders from the front seat. "Lenny, let's keep it flatulence-free for now. Cool?"

I stifle a nervous giggle.

"I'll try," Lenny says, giving Damon a thumbs-up. But as soon as we turn out of the parking lot, I hear Lenny say to Caleb, "Wanna pull my finger?"

I have to look. Instead of pushing Lenny's finger away from his face or, better yet, ignoring him, Caleb grabs Lenny's finger and bends it back.

"Stop it," I tell Caleb as Lenny winces and tries to wrest his hand free. "You're hurting him!"

What happened to Caleb to make him lash out so quickly?

Caleb releases Lenny's finger. Lenny shoots Caleb a look that says he'll retaliate later, then scoots to the other side of the bench.

"You asked for it," Caleb says smugly as Lenny examines his bruised finger.

"I'm gonna sue you if it's sprained," Lenny warns. "I play the guitar, man."

Caleb smirks, then looks at me shaking my head. "What?"

"Nothing," I say.

I turn back around. I won't look at Caleb again. Not until I have to, at least.

Next to me, Matt pulls out his cell phone and starts texting with his one hand. His palm cradles the phone while his thumb taps the keypad. I can't imagine it's easy for him, but he seems to be managing fine.

I lean forward, placing my hands on the seat in front of me. I'll make small talk with Trish and Erin. Anything is better than wondering about Caleb, and because we're going to be living in close quarters for the next month, I need to make friends with these girls. But I realize, pretty quick, that they don't want to chat. Trish puts headphones in her ears and lifts her hoodie to hide her face. Erin is so engrossed in her book I'm not sure she knows that real life is going on around her.

I slump back in my seat and stare out the window. The cornfields and farms outlining the Illinois landscape are a blur.

"Yo, Matt," Caleb says.

"Yeah?"

"Switch seats with me."

THREE
Caleb

I think Maggie still has her mouth open in shock when I climb over the seat and Matt changes places with me. I don't like seeing another guy sitting next to her. I know it's stupid that I feel possessive when I have no right.

Damon glances back. "Caleb, stay in your seat."

"I was getting carsick," I say. "It's either switch seats or puke all over Maggie and Matt."

I look over at Maggie, who doesn't look too happy. She scoots further away from me when our knees touch, but she meets my stare with her own.

"I was carsick," I say dumbly. "And Lenny smells like shit . . . literally. I can't take it."

"I heard that," Lenny says.

"Good," I say back.

Maggie flips her light brown hair back with a confidence I only got glimpses of when we were together. She tosses me a sideways glance. "Why are you trying to start a fight with Lenny?"

"I'm not. *He* started it." I sound like a little kid, but at this point I don't care. What does Maggie think, that I'm perfect? She should know by now that I'm far from it.

"You're being confrontational."

"What's wrong with being confrontational?" I ask.

Maggie puts her regal nose in the air. "I'm sure you can figure that one out on your own."

"Everything okay back there?" Damon pipes in.

"My finger hurts," Lenny blurts out. "I need an ice pack."

I roll my eyes as Damon asks Lenny what happened. After a slight pause and a warning glare from me, Lenny says it's nothing.

Maggie takes out a travel guide of Spain and puts on a pair of wire-rimmed glasses. They must be new, because I haven't seen her with glasses before. She turns away from me and focuses on her book while chewing on the middle of her pencil. I watch as she makes circles on some of the pages and dog-ears others.

"Planning a trip to Spain? Again?" I ask. Right before I left Paradise, she'd said something about changing her mind and not taking her spring semester abroad after all.

She closes the book and shoves it and the gnawed pencil in her backpack. "Yes."

That's it. No details, no explanations. Not that she owes me any. She obviously doesn't want to talk to me, or look at me for that matter.

After two hours, Damon parks the van at a rest stop. "Everyone out. Go to the bathroom and stretch your legs. We'll be eating a quick dinner here."

While we're waiting for everyone else to come back from the bathroom, I walk up to Maggie, who's standing over by the vending machines.

"What's up?" I ask, trying to act normal.

She gives me a look of both disgust and surprise. "*What's up?* Are you kidding me, Caleb? You disappeared for eight months. You've kind of passed the *what's up* stage by seven months."

Shit. I have a feeling nothing I say will be good enough, but I give it a try. "Sorry."

"I'm sorry too." Maggie turns and walks away, her limp a stark reminder of that fateful night two years ago. For a semi-crippled girl, she sure limps away fast. I jog to catch up to her, because I'm stupid and can't leave well enough alone.

"You telling me you haven't thought about us while I was gone?" I ask her.

She shrugs. "I've thought about you. And then I thought about how you left me."

"It wasn't about you, Maggie. You know that."

"I don't want to rehash it," she says as she nears the van. "I've moved on."

I step in front of her, stopping her before she gets too close to the rest of the group. They don't need to know our private business. "You can't ignore me forever."

She shakes her head and pushes me away. "No, I can't ignore you. I couldn't even if I wanted to. But don't try and make me talk about ... us."

She whispers the "us" as if it's a big secret and she doesn't want anyone to know we had a relationship that went beyond a simple friendship.

Back in the van after dinner, she puts her hands in her lap and stares straight ahead as Damon drives us to the campground. After a while, I notice her eyes starting to close.

"You can lean on me if you want to sleep," I offer. "I promise I won't, like, touch you or anything."

"No, thanks. I brought a travel pillow." She reaches into her backpack and pulls out a plastic blow-up fluorescent green airplane pillow. She puffs air into it and wraps it around her neck, just like the Maggie I used to know. Emotional, self-aware Maggie.

She falls asleep almost instantly, and an hour later, everyone except Damon and I are asleep. The girl with the headphones is snoring so loud I wonder if Maggie and the tattooed girl will have to get earplugs before this trip is over.

"Take a nap, Caleb. We've still got a ways to go," Damon says.

"I stopped taking naps when I was two years old," I tell him, stealing another glance at the sleeping Maggie.

I blow out a frustrated breath, then stare at my knee. I'm bouncing it up and down to the rhythm of the van's engine. I'm anxious and don't even know why. I wish I could get up and walk off this nervous energy, or run until my body screams for me to stop. Instead, I'm stuck just sitting here, thinking.

When I was in juvie, I had too much time to think. Thinking too hard and too long is dangerous for anyone with demons they're trying to fight off.

While Maggie sleeps, I envy her. I'm glad she's moved on, but I'm not sure I have. I left Paradise, but I'm the same guy in the same predicament I was in then.

When we finally arrive at the campground, Damon hops out of the van to sign us in. He comes back five minutes later, frowning. "Bad news," he says.

"The campers decided they didn't want to listen to a bunch of sob stories?" I ask.

"No. They only have one unoccupied cabin. That means ..."

"Guys and girls are sleeping in the same cabin?" Tattoo Girl asks.

Damon sighs. He's obviously thrown off by this deviation from his plan. "Yeah. I'll be sleeping in the next cabin, with the counselors. I'll check in on you guys every few hours. Everyone okay with that?"

"Umm, no!" the other girl announces. "I'm not changing in front of guys."

"There's a girls' bathroom just a few feet away from the cabin," Damon informs her. "You can change there, Trish."

"If that's the only option, then I'll live with it," Trish says. "But for the record, I'm not happy about it."

Everyone else is okay with the unexpected sleeping arrangements. Maggie looks a little nervous now that Damon has parked beside the super small cabin. We all pile out.

Inside the barely habitable cabin are three bunk beds, with sheets and pillows at the foot of each mattress but not much else. I worked construction a bunch of summers for my uncle and am pretty sure this place is put together with spit and glue ... and a few nails that popped years ago and nobody bothered to fix.

"I get the bottom bunk," Matt says as he plops himself down onto one of the thin mattresses and sinks almost to the floor. "Damn, Damon, this is roughing it to the max."

"I want a bottom one, too," Trish says.

"Me too," I say, then watch as Maggie limps into the cabin. "On second thought, I'll take a top bunk. Maggie needs a bottom bunk because of her, uh ..."

"Leg?" Maggie finishes for me. "You can say it, Caleb. It's not like it's a secret. Everyone can see I walk with a limp."

"Oh, and while we're talking about obvious imperfections," Matt says, "I might as well announce that I'm aware I have a stump for an arm. It's the obvious white elephant in the room, so I just want y'all to know it's okay to talk about it or ask me questions about it."

"Eww," Trish cries out. "Do you have to call it a stump?"

"Would you rather I call it my partial appendage?" Matt asks, pulling up his sleeve and showing off what remains of his left arm.

She takes a quick look at it. "No."

Damon claps his hands together, getting our attention. "Okay, everyone. Now that that's settled, get situated and then meet me outside in ten minutes."

"Outside?" Trish asks. "For what?"

This girl is definitely going to be in the race with Lenny for the most annoying person in our group. She hasn't smiled or said one remotely positive thing since this trip started. I have a feeling she's trying to make everyone have as miserable a time as she wants to have. Then again, I'm with her—I'd rather be back in Chicago than here.

"Just come outside in ten," Damon says, then pushes open the screen door and disappears.

Tattoo Girl, whose name is Erin, jumps onto the top bunk above Maggie's bed. I take the one above Matt, knowing it doesn't really matter what bed I take because I probably won't fall asleep until I'm so exhausted my body gives in.

After we've organized our stuff, we line up outside. It's starting to get dark, and the mosquitoes are definitely out. We take turns spraying ourselves with repellent while Damon explains how the event will go. "It's casual, so no pressure. Take a deep breath, and know that we're all here to support each other. Since it's late, not all of you will talk tonight, but that's okay. You'll all get a chance to share at some point."

Damon leads us into the woods. About twenty kids are sitting beside a campfire on tree stumps, waiting for us. They all look up when we approach.

The crackling of the wood makes me think back to the time when my dad and I used to go with Brian and his dad camping up in Wisconsin. Last time I talked to Brian, he was dating my ex-girlfriend Kendra and working at his dad's hardware store.

"Take a seat," Damon says to our group. "Pick an empty spot anywhere."

I sit next to this guy with a bunch of acne, who must be a freshman with out-of-control hormones. He smiles weakly at me.

A woman gets up and says the kids are from high schools in the Chicago area and are required to take summer school to move on to the next grade level.

After the woman talks, Damon stands. "I've brought some teens here to tell their stories about how reckless driving has affected their lives. I know some of you think you're invincible, but guess again. Listen to them. Hear their stories. You'll be smarter for it." He sits down.

Silence.

What does he expect us to do, jump up and tell our sob stories? Does he actually think these kids sitting around the fire will give a shit? This is a joke.

Someone coughs.

Someone sneezes.

"Hey, guys. I'm Matt." Matt's voice cuts through the silence. He clears his throat. A few kids look up, but most are picking at their nails or staring into the fire. A few are whispering to each other, totally uninterested in what Matt's about to say. "I guess I'll go first. A few months ago, I was coming home from a high school football game. I was an all-state wide receiver. We'd just beaten our rival team on their turf, and I was stoked. The entire time on the bus back to school, we were joking around. I was feeling good. Damn good." He looks up. "Invincible, even."

Some of the kids are still talking amongst themselves, not giving a shit that poor Matt is pouring his heart out to them. Matt doesn't seem to notice they're not paying attention, or maybe he doesn't care.

"After we got back to school and piled in our cars, I was at a stoplight. A friend of mine was next to me. I revved my engine. He revved his." He pauses. "When the light turned green, I pressed down on that pedal so hard my head jerked back. It was a rush, especially knowing I was leaving my friend in the dust. That's when I lost control of my car. I don't remember much before slamming into the tree, and when I woke up I found out they'd had to amputate my arm. The crushed metal mangled it beyond repair."

As if that isn't enough, Matt struggles out of his T-shirt. Now he's got their undivided attention. A few kids gasp, some cringe, and some stare. His chest is still scarred and he's got less than ten inches of his arm left.

He sits back down. "I'm not feeling so invincible now. Lost any chance of a football scholarship and ... and ... and ..." He swipes at his eyes. "And I'll never be able to catch a football again." He looks up, his expression defiant. "Try putting your pants on using one hand. Just for one day, try doing that simple task with one hand. I can tell you right now, it isn't a piece of cake when you've got one arm. If you want the God's honest truth, it sucks. I wish I could turn back time, but I can't. I made a stupid decision because I thought I was invincible, and I'll pay for it the rest of my life."

He sighs and hangs his head.

Well, that was a downer. Damn. And all along I'd hoped we were gonna roast marshmallows and make s'mores. Some bonfire this turned out to be.

My gaze turns to Maggie. Our eyes meet for an intense moment, but then she breaks the connection quickly and focuses on the ground.

When she looks back up, she says though the strained silence, "I'm Maggie. Almost two years ago I was hit by a car ..."

When she stands, she focuses her accusatory gaze on me. Is she going give it up that I was the one convicted of hitting her? I wasn't the one who did it, but she doesn't know I'm holding that secret. Or, even worse, does she expect me to stand up and say I ran into her while driving drunk? I'd choke on the lie. Dammit, I can't deal with this. Not now.

Before she says another word, I stand and head back to the cabin.

"Caleb, get back here," I hear Damon hiss.

I ignore him and keep walking.

FOUR

Maggie

I pause as Caleb retreats into the darkness, the light of the campfire flickering against his dark shirt. I want him to hear my story. The accident changed my life forever, and if anyone needs to hear my side of it, it's Caleb. He owes it to me to listen. The fact that he picked up and walked away was a slap in the face. It means he doesn't care ... about me, about what happened to me, and about our relationship that he professed to be real.

Feelings of anger and betrayal settle inside me. I take a deep breath and look around at the faces of the teens watching me, waiting for me to explain how teen reckless driving affected my life.

"I still have scars ..." I say, my voice trailing off. I let out a slow breath as I think about the reality of it. "Inside and out. A boy I liked was convicted of hitting me, and he went to jail for it. The sad part is, the accident not only affected the two of us, it affected both our families...and pretty much our small town as well. None of us have been the same since."

A small blonde girl with French braids raises her thin hand. "What about the boy?" she asks. "What happened to him?"

I look over at Damon, leaning against a tree in the back. He thinks Caleb was the one who hit me. "I don't know. I think he blames me for being the reason he went to jail."

"That's stupid," the girl mumbles.

"If you make a mistake, you pay the price," one of their counselors says.

The woman has no clue of the truth...that Caleb didn't make a mistake but paid the price anyway.

Trish stands next. She talks about how she was at a high school party and someone at the party slipped cocaine into her purse. When she got pulled over for speeding and running a red light, she got arrested. The drug charge is on her permanent record, and now every time she applies for a job she has to check the box that she's a convicted felon.

With emotions running high, Damon and the rest of the leaders say it's time to head back to our cabins.

When we reach the cabin, Damon storms inside. "Yo, Becker!" he yells in a deep voice I swear could scare the toughest person. The girls are startled and the guys are practically standing at attention. "Get the hell up!"

Caleb is lying on his bunk, his arm resting behind his head. He's wearing loose sweatpants and no shirt. He sits up, seemingly unfazed. "What's your problem?"

Damon walks right up to the bunk. "Get down here, you smartass."

"Nice language, Damon." Caleb jumps down in one movement and faces Damon straight on. They're about the same height, but Caleb is lean and muscular compared to Damon's bulk.

"Yeah, well, I call it as I see it. Apologize to Maggie for walking off," Damon demands as he gestures in my direction. "It was totally disrespectful and rude."

"Sorry," Caleb mumbles insincerely.

Furious, I nudge Damon aside and stand toe-to-toe with Caleb. It's too bad I'm hyper-aware of the ripples in his bare chest just a few inches away. "Why are you so intent on acting like a jerk?"

Caleb gives a short laugh. "'Cause I am one."

"Why are you doing this?" This isn't the real Caleb, the Caleb I grew up with. This is a hardened, fake representation and I hate it.

"I'm not doing anything. This is me, sweetheart. Take it or leave it."

"What's going on between you two?" Trish asks.

"Nothing," I say to her. "Nothing's going on. Right, Caleb?"

I limp out of the cabin, the loose floorboards creaking beneath my sneakers as I get some needed distance between me and everyone else. When I step into the warm night air, I feel better. As I cling to the railing and awkwardly maneuver myself down the three stairs to the grass, I feel Caleb's presence behind me.

I ignore it, even if my stomach is twisting in knots. I have so much to say that I'm holding back.

"Maggie," Caleb's voice echoes through the night air.

I continue walking. When he catches up to me, I turn on my heel and limp away from him. "Leave me alone," I say over my shoulder.

"What'd you want me to do, listen to you talk about how I hit you with my car while I was drunk, then left you for dead lying in the street, then how I went to jail, then after I came out of jail we started . . . started . . ." He winces and presses his palms to his eyes, as if putting our story into words makes it unbearably real.

"A relationship?" I ask, unfazed.

"Whatever you want to call it. It would never have worked."

"You didn't even give us a chance."

"Your mom hates me. My parents would freak if they saw us together. Hell, Maggie, even Damon warned me away from you. You should have been thankful I left, but it's obvious you're still holding out for something to happen between us."

I walk up to Caleb so close I can almost feel the heat

and energy radiating off him. "You need to get over yourself. What we had was a short fling. I'm so over you it's not even funny."

"Come on, Maggie. Admit there's still a part of you that wants me, even though you keep acting like you've gotten me out of your system. You protest too much."

"I feel nothing for you."

Just when I'm about to step away and go back to the cabin, Caleb reaches out and wraps his fingers around my wrist. "Really?" he says.

I swallow, hard. Those fingers on my wrist are full of reckless energy … I know about those fingers all too well. I get mad at myself for remembering how it felt to have that energy focused on me … those fingers lightly caressed my skin once upon a time. All I should be thinking about is putting him in his place, instead of feeling a connection. But when I look up at him, I forget about everything else because those intense, ice blue eyes that are oh, so unique to Caleb Becker are sucking me in.

I twist my wrist out of his grasp, determined to break whatever spell he has on me once and for all.

I'm walking back to the cabin when I hear Caleb laughing behind me.

I stop and turn around. "What's so funny?" I demand. I hope I don't have toilet paper on my shoe or gum on the back of my jeans.

Caleb's laugh turns into a cocky grin. "I figured it out."

"Figured what out?"

"Why you're so adamant about letting me know it's over between us." He crosses his arms on his chest. "It's because you're trying to convince *yourself* it's over. But you and I both know there's something still going on between us."

"You're delusional. The only thing going on between us is hatred and resentment. And I'm not just talking about me here. You resent me just as much as I resent you."

When he steps forward, I take a step back. "You sure?" he asks, his expression even more cocky.

"Yeah. I'm sure," I tell him. "One hundred and *fifty* percent sure."

"Then prove it."

I narrow my eyes at him and wonder what he's up to. "How?"

"Kiss me, Maggie. Right here, right now."

FIVE

Caleb

"**O**ne kiss," I say, and step closer. "If you're so over me, then it won't be a big deal."

She puts her nose in the air. She has no clue how watching her act like she's a tough chick makes me want to get under her skin even more. I'm not sure of my motives... I don't want to think about it too hard for fear I might actually come up with answers.

"I don't kiss guys just to prove things," she declares with an attitude I've only seen her put on a few times. "And I especially don't have to prove anything to you."

She doesn't want to admit we've still got something between us. It's simmering beneath the surface of hatred and resentment, or whatever the hell she wants to label it.

As much as I want to keep my distance, at the same time I want to see how far I can take it. Testing her is a bad idea; I know that. It's good if she's over me. But I can't resist—I've got to know for sure. "What are you afraid of? If you're really done with me then our kiss won't mean anything and you can move on."

"I *have* moved on, Caleb. But if you really want me to prove it to you, I will."

I paste a mischievous smile on my face. "Bring it on."

The old Maggie would have blushed and stared at the ground in the face of being challenged. The old Maggie would have turned and run. She used to be predictable. Now she's not, and it's throwing me off my game.

The new Maggie, the Maggie who puts me in my place and gets under *my* skin, reaches out and steadies herself by putting her palm on my chest. She tilts her head back and gazes up at me, her chameleon eyes shining a dark gray in the moonlight. "You shouldn't challenge me," she says.

"I know," I say, careful to keep my voice even and cool.

Having her this close makes my body so aware and alive I have to fight to keep myself in check. My heart is racing and my senses are heightened so much that I can smell her flowery perfume from the short distance between us. I hope and pray she doesn't realize the powerful effect she still has on me. I haven't felt like this since, well, that night in Mrs. Reynolds' gazebo when I wanted her more than I've ever wanted any girl. It ended innocently, but man I wanted to take it to the next level ... or even further.

While I'm sure Maggie can feel my heart beating hard and fast against her palm right now, I try and forget it as she reaches up and weaves her hand in my hair.

"You ready?" I ask in a gravelly voice.

"Sure," she says tentatively as I bend my head down. I want to put my hand on her cheek and feel her soft skin beneath my fingers, or brush away the stray hair that's fallen in her eyes. But I don't. It would be too intimate and break what little control I have. My lips hover over hers, teasing. I want her to want this as much as I do.

"Just don't tell anyone, okay?" she warns, pulling back the slightest bit.

Those words deflate my libido as fast as it was fired up.

Don't tell anyone? Okay, to be honest I'm not surprised she doesn't want to let anyone know about our private little moment of truth or dare. But at the same time her words cut. She doesn't want anyone to know because she likes another guy? Or because she's suddenly embarrassed of being associated with an ex-con? Shit, maybe she really is over me. Reality, like a tidal wave, washes over me.

What the hell am I doing? I can't do this. When we got together back in Paradise, nothing was calculated. It just happened. But now, this entire scene is a challenge, a total setup. Being emotionally involved with any girl, *especially* Maggie, is the last thing I need. And that's where this is leading to.

Maybe I just need to get laid. Maybe I just need a one night stand with some ditz like Trish in an attempt to wipe

Maggie from my thoughts. A one night stand right now would probably restore my sanity.

I take my hands off Maggie and step back. I shrug and give her a cocky glare. "You're right," I say. "This is stupid. You don't have to prove anything to me."

I can't tell if she's relieved or disappointed. It doesn't matter, really. I don't want to wait around while she analyzes what just did, or didn't, happen. I don't want to analyze it, either.

I leave her standing alone and walk toward the fire pit. I hear her call my name but keep going, worried I'll lose my resolve, take back my words, and kiss her like no other guy would. Hurrying down the moonlit, wooded path to increase the distance between us, I finally reach the clearing. The fire is almost out, except for a few stubborn embers.

I sit on one of the benches, which is really just a wooden log tossed on the ground. Less than an hour ago, in this same exact spot, Maggie shared our story. She still doesn't have a clue about what really happened the night of the accident. The story she tells is truth to her, but a total fabrication that I've lived with for a long time now.

I sit by the fire until the last struggling ember dies. When I finally go back to the cabin, all the lights are out except for the few leading to the restrooms. Inside the cabin, everyone seems to be sleeping or, in Trish's case, snoring a barnyard symphony. Even Maggie is out, although her back is to me and I can't see her face. The sheet covering her is moving up and down, slowly and rhythmically, with each breath.

I rummage through my duffle. For a brief moment I wonder where Damon is, then remember he's crashed out in the air-conditioned counselors' cabin with real beds while we're stuck here roughing it "to the max," as Matt had pointed out earlier.

After washing up, I hop on my top bunk, careful not to wake Matt although the metal bunk and springs creak loudly as I settle into the mattress. When I hear Matt stir, I mumble, "Sorry, dude."

"No prob," he whispers. "I wasn't really sleeping anyway."

"Who can sleep when we've got Trish the fuckin' bulldozer in here with us?" Lenny cries out, then growls in frustration.

As if on cue, Trish's snoring increases in tone and volume. It's not one of those heavy breathing jobs, either. First she starts gurgling as if she's storing phlegm in the back of her throat. Then she lets out a symphony of snorting and gurgling noises I've never in my life heard before, even from a guy.

Lenny, who's sleeping above Trish, leans down to look at her. "Trish, shut the fuck up!" he practically yells.

Trish doesn't stir. She does stop snoring for half a second, but then starts up again, even louder than before.

"I can suffocate her with my pillow," Lenny offers as an option.

Matt sits up. "I hear if you put someone's hand in warm water while they're sleeping they stop snoring."

"That's to make someone pee in their bed," I tell him.

"Does it really work?" Lenny asks, obviously excited. "We should try it. Who's got a bucket?"

"You're kidding, right?" Maggie chimes in from below in a low whisper. "You can't do that."

A big snort comes out of Trish's open mouth. Lenny sits up, grabs both sides of the top bunk, and starts rocking the bed from side to side.

"Don't do that!" Maggie shrieks.

Hearing Maggie shrieking makes me jump off the bed just in time to see Lenny and Trish's bunk start to tip over. As the metal is about to crash on metal, I reach out and grab the bed frame before it collides with Maggie's bunk and Maggie. Her leg is damaged enough as it is. My leg stops Trish, but it's too late for Lenny, who falls with a huge thump.

Trish slowly slides down my leg and lands ass-first in a puddle of tangled sheets on the floor. She looks up, startled and scared. For a girl who I assume prides herself on looking tough as nails, startled and scared doesn't fit.

"What happened?" she asks, her eyes wide as I make sure her bed is upright and stable again. She stands, then rubs her butt a few times before scooping up her sheets and pillow.

It's obvious Lenny isn't gonna explain, so I offer a quick explanation. "Your bed fell over. Go back to sleep."

"How did it fall over?" she asks, dumping her armload back onto the bed.

"Holy shit, that was awesome!" Lenny cries out from

the floor. He's laughing, as if scaring the girls half to death was crazy fun. He's a moron.

"Dude, get a grip," I tell him.

Trish narrows her eyes at Lenny. "Did you tip the bunk on purpose?"

"You were snoring like a fuckin' pig, Trish. I tried to wake you, but you sleep like the dead. I was doin' us all a favor."

Like an attack dog, Trish lunges at Lenny. I catch her just in time and hold her back. "You're an asshole!" she yells at Lenny.

"Tell me what I don't know," Lenny responds, then snorts loudly like a pig to piss her off. If he didn't notice, the girl has some scary-ass fingernails. They're long, they're pointy, they're digging into my arms now, and I have no doubt Trish will use them as weapons the first chance she gets. The last thing I would do is set her off and have those claws come out slashing.

"Trish, don't let him get to you," Maggie says calmly as she gets between Trish and Lenny. Maggie is wearing a pink tank top and matching pajama bottoms that cover just about everything. I'm all too aware that if Trish lunges again, Maggie could easily fall and hurt her leg. "Caleb, let her go."

I release Trish slowly, ready to grab her again if I sense she's about to pounce. Maggie stays between her and Lenny, who finally stops laughing.

Everyone is awake now, all of us glaring at Lenny.

"You losers have no sense of humor," Lenny complains. He moons us with his hairy ass before stomping out of the cabin.

Erin shrieks, then pulls her sheet above her head.

"I'm not sleeping below that jerk," Trish declares.

"I'll sleep below him," I offer. "Take my bed." Trish seems too tired and pissed to be thankful as she climbs onto my mattress.

I sit on the rumpled pile of bedding on Trish's bed and realize now I'll be sleeping right next to Maggie. I look at her. I didn't notice before, but now it's plain to see that Maggie isn't wearing a bra. While I'm sitting on the bunk and she's standing next to me her breasts are at eye level. I hear her suck in a breath.

She points to my hand and whispers, "You're *bleeding*."

I look down. Sure enough, blood is dripping off the back of my hand. I guess when I stuck my hand between the metal bunks it got cut. I wipe the blood off on my shorts. "It's not a big deal."

Maggie furrows her eyebrows as she pulls a towel out of her suitcase and hands it to me. "Here."

"I'm not messing up your towel with my blood," I tell her, tossing it back.

She catches it with one hand, then rolls her eyes and sighs. "You can stop playing the hero at any time, you know."

"You think I'm a hero?"

"No comment," she says as she grabs my wrist and

pulls my hand toward her so she can examine the cut. Her face is tense and stern as she dabs her towel on my hand. Reaching into her backpack, she pulls out a water bottle. She pours water on the towel, then continues to clean the cut. It stings, but I don't make a sound. I can't even remember the last time someone actually took care of me, and it feels foreign. I shift on the bed, feeling uncomfortable. I'm used to being alone and taking care of myself. I've never played the needy guy before, and I'm not about to now. Especially in front of Maggie.

I pull my hand back. "I'm fine."

Maggie *tsks* and bends down so we're face to face. Her gaze meets mine. "No, you're not."

I need to turn the tables or lose whatever control I have when it comes to me and Maggie. My resolve to push her away is weak as it is. I better step up and be the guy she thinks I've become.

"Are you bending over like that on purpose?" I ask her as I gesture toward her chest. "'Cause I've got damn good view of your tits right about now."

SIX

Maggie

At Caleb's words, I straighten and cross my arms over my chest to prevent further ogling. "You're disgusting," I whisper, hoping nobody else heard his crass remark.

"Thanks," he responds.

I slide under my covers, unwilling to look in Caleb's direction. "Bleed to death for all I care."

"Want your towel back?" he asks, his cocky attitude out in full force. Why does he do that? One minute I feel like he's being his true self, the Caleb I once knew, and the next minute he acts like the guy he wants everyone to think he is.

"No."

"Will you two quit flirting already?" Trish chimes in.

"Either admit you guys have a thing for each other or go to bed. Or both."

"I don't have a thing for him," I declare.

"You used to," I hear Caleb mutter under his breath from his bed beside me.

"Ancient history. Didn't I tell you I moved on?" I mutter back.

"Go to sleep, Maggie," Caleb says roughly. "You're getting repetitive."

I turn my back to him. So what if I keep insisting it's over? It's true. If I'm completely honest, I guess a part of me still yearns for the way things were when we were together. But I know he's the last thing I need in my life, and it's obvious Caleb and I are on the same page in that respect. He's been trying to push me away by goading me, and he's doing a great job of it.

When my body finally relaxes and I feel like I'm drifting off, Trish starts snoring again.

I glance at Caleb. He's lying on his back, wrapped in a wadded-up sheet, with his arms folded behind his head. He's obviously not sleeping. As if feeling my gaze on him, he turns to look at me. The bunks aren't that far apart, and if I reached out I could touch his bare shoulder.

He sighs and slightly shakes his head, then looks away. I turn on my back and focus on the squeaking springs above me, wondering how I got here. When I got the call from my physical therapist asking if I wanted to be part of this program, I really felt like it was my chance to close this chapter of my life. I thought if I could share my experience with others instead of keeping all my feelings bottled up inside me, I could make the accident a part of my past and be able to look forward to the future.

I wish Caleb felt the same way and could put our ugly past behind us. To be honest, though, I don't think he'll get past it until he admits the truth.

The truth.

He has no clue that I know he didn't hit me with that car. I've been itching to tell him I know the truth.

But I can't. He's obviously keeping up the facade for a reason.

I force myself to fall asleep and forget that Caleb is sleeping next to me.

In the morning, when I'm walking back from the bathroom on the gravel path that leads to our cabin, I find Lenny sleeping soundly in a patch of grass. He's snoring so loud the sound echoes through the entire campground. I suppress a laugh. He could definitely give Trish a run for her money in the snoring department.

Damon is waiting inside the cabin. "Can someone tell me why Lenny is sleeping outside instead of in a bed?" he demands.

"Maybe he wanted to sleep with his relatives?" Trish says, shrugging.

Damon doesn't look happy. "Not funny. His face already looks like a tomato from the morning sun beating down on him and there are a crapload of mosquito bites on him. Someone wake him up. Now."

"I'll do it," Caleb says.

"I'll go with you," Matt offers and the two boys leave the cabin.

When the three boys walk back in the cabin a few minutes later, one good look at Lenny and my mouth drops open. I didn't realize it as I walked past him this morning, but Damon was right. Lenny's face is bright red and totally sunburned. Mosquito bites are scattered on his face and body.

Lenny points at each and every one of us and says in a warning tone, "Don't. Say. Anything."

"What the hell happened to you?" Damon asks Caleb as he gestures to the dried blood now caked on Caleb's hand. Damon is totally confused.

"One of the beds tipped over last night," Erin chimes in. "Caleb caught it before it crashed on Maggie and me."

I think the rest of us are shocked Erin actually spoke—she's been so quiet.

"*Lenny* tipped the bed," Trish says. "*On purpose.*"

Lenny sneers at Trish. "Do you know what they do in jail to people who snitch?"

"Lenny, I won't tolerate threats so knock it off. Follow me to the infirmary. Caleb, you too. I want your hand checked out. The rest of you, pack up the van and go to breakfast. The dining hall is the big building by the front office."

When we're all ready, Damon, Lenny and Caleb head for the infirmary while the rest do as instructed. The dining hall is a huge building with rows of picnic tables. At the end of the room, teens line up with trays and choose their food.

"So what's the real story with you and Caleb?" Matt asks me as we join the line.

I wonder how much I should reveal. "It's super-complicated." I grab a carton of milk and look at Matt. "Need help?" I ask when he picks up a tray and balances it on his arm.

"I got it," he says.

I really admire Matt for that.

I watch him balance his tray steadily on his functional arm while we pick our breakfasts and head to one of the tables to eat.

"Nice way to avoid the question about Caleb, Maggie."

"I'm not avoiding it," I tell him.

He raises an eyebrow, obviously not convinced.

Trish and Erin sit down opposite us. What should I say? How much should I tell Matt? This trip is supposed to be about not holding back and letting it all out. Caleb hasn't been truthful with me or anyone else...and I feel like it's eating away at him. I won't let it eat at me.

I turn to Matt. "Caleb and I were involved after he was released from juvie."

"Wow."

I watch Matt's reaction go from shocked to curious. The accident and the consequences connect me and Caleb forever, whether we want it to or not. But Matt doesn't know the entire story. Damon, the guy who's supposed to know everything about each Re-START participant, doesn't even know the entire story.

"What did he go to juvie for?" Matt asks.

"Umm …" I take a second to figure out what to say, how to put it into words.

"Tell him, Maggie," Caleb says, sticking his head between us. "Spill it." Before I can even answer, Caleb snaps, "For hitting Maggie while driving drunk."

Matt's mouth opens wide in shock. "Holy shit. For real?"

"For real. Right, Maggie?" Caleb narrows his eyes at me as if I betrayed him. "Why don't we announce it to the entire room?"

"No."

"Come on, Mags. Be adventurous."

"You're not serious," I say.

He clears his throat. "Watch me."

SEVEN

Caleb

I wasn't really gonna tell everyone in this damn place that I'd gone to juvie, but seeing Maggie on this let's-share-absolutely-everything kick pisses me off. This Re-START program is a bunch of crap. They think talking about the accident will miraculously fix everything. I have news for Damon and everyone else involved. *Nothing* will fix my shitty life. *Nothing* will erase the past two years. *Nothing* will change the fact that I've got no friends or family left. I'm just living...surviving, really.

Finding Maggie in an intense conversation with Matt made me want to grab the guy's shirt and pick a fight with him. The guy is cool, unlike that tool Lenny, but when I moved in closer and found Maggie confiding in him, my veins fired up.

I scan the room and eye a bullhorn by the front door. "Caleb, don't," Maggie says.

I ignore her as I cross the room and pick up the bullhorn. I click the siren switch. An obnoxiously loud, piercing shriek echoes throughout the building—a good thing, because everyone immediately has their attention focused on me.

I bring the bullhorn to my lips. "I've got something to say," I bellow into the mouthpiece.

Damon is standing in line with a tray full of food. I expect him to run up to me and grab the bullhorn out of my hand, but he doesn't. Instead, he puts down his tray and nods for me to continue.

"I drove home drunk from a high school party," I say, my voice sounding foreign to me as the words flow out through the bullhorn. "I hit a girl, and left her lying in the street not knowing if she was dead or alive. I was a jock, a guy who'd probably get a wrestling scholarship to college and I didn't want to screw that up. So I ditched her. In the end, I was busted and went to jail for a year."

I unclick the sound button. The place is silent. I can imagine what I must look like...the cool high school jock boy who screwed up and is now whining about it. Nobody is gonna feel sorry for me, not that I want or expect them to.

When I look over at Maggie, she shakes her head and turns her back on me. She's shutting me out once again, but I don't care.

I press the talk button again. "When I came out of jail, I got involved with my victim."

More than a few teens in the room go wide-eyed at this new piece of information. They're whispering in shock and pointing at me.

"We kissed, we fooled around…she snuck me in her house and we *slept* together. People warned me not to get involved with her, but I did. Biggest mistake of my life."

Out of the corner of my eye, I watch as Maggie slides off the bench and heads for the swinging doors. Good ol' Matt follows her.

"Maggie!" I say through the bullhorn. She flinches and stops in her tracks. "You want to add something? I skipped the part when we were in Mrs. Reynolds' gazebo."

I follow Maggie, who thinks that talking is better than keeping your mouth shut. I hope I've changed her mind, and she realizes that living in La-La Land is better than facing reality.

"That's the girl I'm talking about," I say, pointing.

"Shut up, Caleb," she hisses at me.

I hand her the bullhorn. "Truth hurts, huh?"

EIGHT

Maggie

We're back in the van headed to our next destination, Freeman University. After the dining room incident, I hobbled far into the woods and cried. Matt followed me. He didn't ask whether Caleb's statements were true or not... he just stood there while tears rolled down my face and I wiped them with the back of my hand.

Caleb's little show this morning was beyond obnoxious.

He lied.

He twisted the truth.

He mocked me, and he mocked whatever relationship we'd had.

Taunting me to reveal what happened between us in Mrs. Reynolds' gazebo was too much for me. That night

Caleb and I shared precious private moments I'll remember for the rest of my life. It was perfect; from the twinkling lights he'd carefully wrapped around the entire gazebo to the romantic way he kissed me after I slow danced in his arms. He treated me like I was the only girl in the world who mattered, and the only girl he'd ever want to be with.

This morning, he tainted my memory of that night forever.

Thank goodness Damon ordered Caleb to sit in the passenger seat. I don't think he's too happy with Caleb right now. I'm not, either.

We park at Dixon Hall, one of the Freeman University dorms. It's across from a big brick library with floor-to-ceiling windows.

Damon leads us to a suite on the second floor of the dorm. It's got a kitchen with a table, and two couches in the common living room area. "Girls in that bedroom," Damon says as he points to a door. "Guys in the other." He smiles as he tosses his suitcase into the third room, closest to the couches. "I get this room for myself."

"How long are we staying here?" Matt asks.

"This will be our home base for a while," Damon tells him. "We'll be taking day trips from here."

"My face hurts," Lenny complains. "And it itches." He resembles a mime, with all the white cream the nurse put on him from his sunburn and bites. He walks up to Trish and sticks his face close to hers. "Scratch me."

Trish sneers at him, looking like she'd rather die than

touch his cream-covered face. "Get out of my face, you freak."

"Enough, you two," Damon says sternly. "Trish, I'm not fond of name-calling. Lenny, if you've got an itch, scratch it yourself please."

Erin looks like she's going to throw up just looking at Lenny's cream-colored face.

Lenny walks to the window overlooking the grassy courtyard below. "Check this out, Caleb! Hot college chicks laying out in bikinis."

Ignoring him, Caleb heads for the guys' bedroom with his duffle.

"Get settled, guys," Damon says as he walks into his own room. "I want to have a group meeting in a half hour."

"Great," Caleb mutters sarcastically from the doorway to the guys' room. "Just what I need."

Damon swings around. "You do need it. And before you ask to get out of it, you'll participate just like everyone else." His tone makes clear this is nonnegotiable.

Trish, Erin, and I pick our beds in the girls' room.

"Erin, how come you don't talk?" Trish demands.

Erin shrugs as she unpacks her suitcase and hangs her clothes in the small closet.

"You know this trip is supposed to be about sharing your experiences, right? What did you do, besides get too many tattoos on your arms?"

Erin doesn't answer. She fidgets with a shirt she's trying to fold and put in one of the drawers.

"Leave her alone, Trish," I say. "She'll talk when she wants to."

"Okay, if that's the way it's gonna be, that's fine," Trish says, giving up. "But just so you know, I'm not gonna pretend to be all buddy-buddy if you hold back on me."

I think Erin will stay silent like usual, until her hands still and she turns to us. Her eyes are glassy, as if she's holding back tears.

"My boyfriend is in jail for three years for killing someone in a drive-by. My parents kicked me out of the house. And..." She wipes at her eyes and says in a soft voice, "I'm pregnant."

"Holy crap," Trish says. "No wonder you don't talk."

I elbow Trish in the ribs, hoping she'll get the hint and not say anything that will upset Erin. She's pregnant? With a boy who'll be in jail for three years? Hearing her story makes my problem with Caleb seem about as important as a hangnail.

"If you need anything, we're here for you," I tell her. "Right, Trish?"

"Yeah," Trish is quick to say. I think Erin just earned Trish's loyalty by sharing her story. Maybe Trish practically forcing Erin to talk was a good thing.

"And what about you?" Trish says, turning to me.

I lift my head from my suitcase. I must look like a deer in headlights. "What about me? I told my story at the campfire last night."

"Not about the accident. Caleb said something today about you and him in a gazebo. Care to go into details?"

I quickly shake my head. "Maybe later. We don't want to be late for Damon's meeting." I shove a stack of my clothes into a drawer.

"I think you're stalling."

"You're right, Trish," I say. "I don't want to talk about it."

"Suit yourself." Trish opens the closet door and looks confused. "Wait, where's the bathroom?" she asks as she holds out a plastic bag with her toiletries.

"In the common area, I guess," Erin offers. "We're probably sharing one."

Trish shakes her head as if she heard wrong. "No way. All seven of us can't share one bathroom."

She hurries out to the common area to investigate. Erin and I follow her. Sure enough, there's a bathroom between the guys' room and Damon's room.

Damon comes out of his room. "What's going on?"

"Damon, did you know there's only one bathroom for *all seven* of us?" Trish asks.

Damon shakes his head. "That's not true."

You can feel the sigh of relief from Trish, Erin, and I...until Damon says, "*I* have my own bathroom. Only the six of you have to share one."

Trish puts her hands on her hips. "That's not fair."

Damon chuckles. "Didn't anyone tell you that nothing in life is fair, Trish?"

She peeks her head inside the common bathroom. "Eww!" She points to the toilet. "The seat is up. And there are little droplets of pee and stray pubes on the ring. That's *not* okay."

As if on cue, all three guys join us. "What's the problem?" Matt asks Trish.

"The *problem* is that six of us have to share a bathroom." She glares in the direction of our leader. "And Prince Damon gets his own throne to sit on."

"This isn't a luxury hotel," Lenny informs Trish. "Anyway, what's wrong with the bathroom? It looked fine to me."

Trish gets in Lenny's face. "So you're the culprit. You were in the bathroom."

Lenny shrugs. "So what if I was?"

"Haven't you ever heard the phrase, *If you sprinkle when you tinkle please be neat and wipe the seat?* That goes for stray pubes, as well."

"Haven't you ever heard the phrase, *Shut the fuck up, bitch?*" Lenny fires back.

"I think it's time we have our meeting," Damon says. "Right now."

I avoid eye contact with Caleb as I pick a seat on one of the couches. Trish and Erin sit on either side of me. The guys sit on the opposite couch from the girls.

Damon pulls over a chair from the kitchen table. He takes a deep breath and claps his hands. "Okay, kids, here's the deal. Some rules have to be set, 'cause you guys are drivin' me nuts. First of all, let's try to eliminate the profanity flying out of your mouths. Second, there's to be no consumption of drugs or alcohol. We're on a college campus and I've no doubt they're easy to find. Third, I'm tired of the bickering. It's giving me a headache."

"But—" Trish starts to say, but Damon holds a hand up and stops her from talking.

"About the bathroom situation. You all have to share the one bathroom. Deal with it. There's another bathroom at the end of the hall right next to the elevators if you need it. Guys, put the seat down after you do your thing. Girls, make sure there are no feminine products lying around. Are all we all cool about that?"

We all nod.

"Where are the air-conditioning controls?" Lenny asks. "I'm sweating my butt off in this sauna."

"There is no air conditioning, Lenny. Like you pointed out, this isn't a luxury hotel. Any more questions?"

When nobody answers, Damon says, "Great." He sighs as if a weight has been lifted off him. "Now that that's settled, I've got one more thing. We had some drama this morning thanks to Caleb, and I want to talk about it."

"How 'bout we don't talk about it," Caleb mumbles. "Hell, I'd rather talk about Lenny's pubes."

I'd rather talk about Lenny's pubic hair loss issues, too. It's better than having Caleb and me actually talk about our past... or talk to one another. I'm not going to do it. Not now, when his insults are so raw.

A wave of numbness washes over me. I stand. "I'm sorry, Damon. I just can't. I don't mean to disrespect this group, or this process. I just... need time."

I intentionally look away from Caleb and I'm all too aware of my limp and his nearness as I head to my room and close the door. I don't lock it, though, since I'm sharing it with two other girls.

When I hear a knock as I sit on my bed, I flinch.

"It's Matt. Can I come in?"

"Sure."

Matt opens the door. "Wanna talk?"

"Not really. Is Damon mad?"

"No. He wanted to see if you were okay, but I volunteered to come instead."

"Thanks," I mumble. "I feel bad I just left in the middle of the meeting."

"Don't feel bad," he tells me. "I think everyone understands. Well, except Caleb."

"Why? What did he say?"

Matt comes in the room and stands beside my bed. "He didn't say anything. He just got up and walked out."

NINE

Caleb

I wish Damon hadn't followed me out of the suite. I hear his thundering footsteps behind me before he grabs my shoulder and pulls me around to face him.

"Leave me alone," I tell him, my fists tight and ready to lash out.

"You can't just leave every time the going gets tough, Caleb."

"Watch me," I say roughly as a couple of college guys pass us.

"You want out of the program? You want to go to jail?"

"Is that a threat?"

"Don't test me, Caleb. And give me a damn break. I've got to deal with Trish and Lenny. That alone could give a guy a coronary."

I let out a breath and look away from him. "Give me a damn break, man. I just want to be alone."

"Being alone isn't good."

"It is for me." It's better than watching Matt and Maggie start a relationship right in front of my eyes. The way he ran after her when she fled from the lounge made me sick. I don't blame the guy... but I sure as hell don't need to see it. "I'm stuck here, I get it. I don't have a choice. But can you give me a night off from being around everyone? One night, Damon. It won't kill you... or me." I let out a breath and say quietly, "*Please*."

My transition counselor, the guy who's always been a hardass and whose job was to force me on the straight and narrow, steps back. "Fine."

I'm shocked. Maybe I didn't hear right. "What does that mean?"

"It means I'll give you a pass... for tonight; a pass to be alone and figure things out. I'm taking the rest of the group to dinner with a local youth group and then to a movie."

A night without having to be stoic and pretend I'm a rock is a fucking miracle. A night without having to share my secrets makes me feel like a free man. "Thanks," I say.

"No problem. But tomorrow I expect you to put a damn smile on that mug of yours and suck it up. Got it?"

"Yeah. Yeah, I got it."

Feeling like the noose is loosened, I follow Damon back to the suite. Maybe I should apologize to Maggie for this morning. I knew I'd hurt her with the gazebo comment. We'd made out like crazy that night. Nobody knew about our secret time together except maybe old Mrs. Reynolds, who'd gone to bed after dinner. I think she knew Maggie and I were getting it on, and I've got a feeling she didn't care. Hell, maybe in a way it helped us get over all the shit we'd been going through.

Problem is, the night in the gazebo ended with me trying to ease Maggie's skirt up so I could see her scars. Maggie pushed my hand away. She didn't trust me. The night kind of went downhill from there.

In the suite, Erin and Trish are in the lounge area. I peek into the girls' room. Having Maggie mad at me isn't my intention.

Maggie is lying on one of the beds. Matt is sitting on the bed next to her. They're obviously in an intimate conversation, because they're alone and whispering. Oh, hell.

I retreat and head back to the guys' room, glad they didn't catch me watching them. Lenny is sitting on his bed, wearing nothing but his skimpy briefs. He's holding a personal mini-fan up to his chest.

"You do know the girls can walk in here at any second, don't you?"

The door wasn't closed or locked. Trish and Erin are sitting right outside the door, and if they crane their necks they'd probably have a good view of Lenny practically naked.

"I don't give a shit, Caleb. I'm fucking hot as hell."

He proceeds to lift up the band of his briefs and faces the mini-fan toward his dick. "My poor ball sacks are sweatin' so bad I swear I won't be able to have kids. My boys are being cooked to death in there."

"Might be a good thing. I'm not sure you should be allowed to procreate anyway," I murmur as I turn away. I'm glad Damon isn't making me go to dinner with the group, 'cause getting a glimpse of Lenny fanning his sweaty nuts made me lose my appetite.

Seeing Maggie and Matt talking on her bed hasn't helped my appetite or mood, either.

"Just an FYI," Lenny says, his face still red from the nasty sunburn. "I've got a shitload of condoms in my duffle. Front pocket."

"For what?"

"Listen, if you don't know what condoms are for I'm not gonna teach you."

"I know what they're for, shithead. I just highly doubt you're getting any ass on this trip."

"Watch me," Lenny says. "My boy gets action all the time."

"Yeah, I bet your right hand is tired from all that action," I mumble as I walk to the bathroom.

"I'm a leftie!" Lenny calls after me. I try not to wince from thinking about it.

I take a quick shower to cool off, then change into jeans and a T-shirt. I don't have a chance to explain or apologize to Maggie, because she's too busy talking with Matt.

Thing is, they deserve each other. Matt's a decent guy. I can't blame him for going for her. Maggie might not be the girl who stands out in a crowd or the one with a model's body, but once you get to know her, I mean really know her, you just see her...a girl who wears her heart on her sleeve and is so genuine you're afraid every word out of your mouth will come out wrong. She's someone you don't have to worry will cheat on you, like my ex Kendra did. Maggie is—

I've got to stop thinking about her. It's like I'm torturing myself for no reason except to piss myself off.

After the group leaves for dinner and whatever additional festivities Damon has planned, I need some air. The suite is too hot even with the windows wide open.

I walk through the tree-lined Freeman University campus, trying not to think about how I got here and what I'll be doing after this program is finished. I've got nothing to look forward to.

I walk past a bunch of guys playing football on the quad. The quarterback has no aim and the ball flies right in my direction.

I catch it.

"Nice catch," one guy says. "We could use another receiver. Wanna play?"

"Sure," I say, shrugging.

I join one of the teams and play with them until it's too dark to see the ball and one of the guys tells the others they're late for their own frat party.

"What's your name?" the quarterback asks me as we walk off their makeshift field.

"Caleb."

"I'm David. Listen, Caleb. My buddies and I are having a little get-together at our frat house. Come with us."

"Yeah. Come on," one of the other guys says as he tosses the football in the air. "It's the least we could do for having you help us kick Garrett's ass on the field today."

"That was suh-weet!" the quarterback agrees, and they give each other an enthusiastic high-five.

I follow the guys two blocks until we reach their fraternity house. It's impressive—a massive three-story house with four white columns in front. It looks like a damn mansion. A bunch of girls and guys are hanging on the front porch. Music blares from inside.

As soon as I walk in with David and the other guys, I realize their little party isn't a little party. It's a big one, and it's in full swing.

Before I know it, David shoves a red plastic cup in my hand. "So, Caleb, you a freshman? Haven't seen you around FU before."

"I'm not really a student," I say, then take a sip of whatever's in the cup. Beer. Cold beer. I'm sure Damon had some rule about drinking, but the alcohol tastes so good going down my throat that I'm not about to toss it. The fact that I know the more I drink the more I'll stop thinking about Maggie and Matt sitting on her bed this afternoon deep in conversation is a bonus. "I'm staying in the dorms for a stupid program I got stuck on."

"I hate stupid programs," David says.

"Hey, Davie," says a blonde girl with a short skirt and low-cut top. She finishes off the beer in her plastic cup, and I get the distinct feeling she started partying way before us. "Who's your hot friend?"

David drapes his arm on the girl's shoulders. "Caleb, this is Brandi. She's one of our frat house neighbors and our resident babe. Brandi, show my man Caleb here a good time." He excuses himself with a wink to me.

The girl looks me up and down, then flashes me a wide smile with a peek of tongue showing.

"Wanna dance?" she asks.

I finish what's left in my cup. "Sure."

She takes my hand and leads me to a crowded room off to the side. There's a keg and we both fill up our cups. Cup in hand, she starts moving her sexy body to the music. I hastily gulp my beer down and walk toward her. Our bodies grind together with the beat of the music, and one thought goes through my mind: tonight I need this girl.

TEN

Maggie

"Where's Caleb?" I ask Damon as we walk to the pizza place a few blocks away from the campus. He said a high school youth group is meeting us there, so their members can talk to us and hear our stories.

"He's gonna stay in tonight," Damon says. "I think he needs time to cool off and think about why he's here."

I sigh, knowing the truth of it all. "He doesn't want to be a part of this group."

"Yeah, well, he needs to be here nonetheless," Damon says as his cell rings. "He just needs to get a grip on his emotions."

As Damon takes the call, Matt is at my side. "You okay?" he asks.

I nod. "I'm kind of glad Caleb isn't coming with us."

"Me too."

I flash Matt a questioning look. "Why?"

"'Cause you seem upset when he's around." He shrugs sheepishly. "I don't like seeing you upset."

I put my arm around Matt and smile up at him. "Thanks for being a good friend," I say, leaning into his chest as we follow the others.

He puts his arm around me. "No prob."

It's nice knowing I have Matt here. During physical therapy we'd talk a bit, and complain about Robert, our physical therapist. Robert loves to push his patients to the limit whether they like it or not.

"Caleb's not such a bad guy," I tell him.

"I know," Matt says. "Caleb's cool. All of us have screwed-up shit we have to work out. Caleb just seems to have sunk deeper than we have."

"You seem to be handling your problems better than most of us on this trip," I tell him.

"I fake it. Truth is, I'm glad I'm here, but I've got to admit that some of those kids last night looked at me like I was a complete moron." He pauses, then adds, "Then again, I *was* a complete moron, but it's like going through it all over again. I wonder if I'll ever get used to the looks and the stares."

"I won't," I admit to him. "At first I was super self-conscious whenever I'd walk into a room ... I noticed all eyes on me. I still get the pity stares, which might be worse than your moron stares."

"Come on, Maggie. We both have obvious disabilities, unlike the rest on this trip. And we're both trying to get over our past relationships."

Matt stops and lets the others go ahead of us. "Can you imagine *us* as a couple?" he asks me.

I'm not sure if he's wondering how people would react to seeing a limping girl and one-armed boy together, or if he really is wondering if I could imagine dating him.

I've never thought about it before.

Matt's sweet.

He's cute.

He's a good guy.

But...

"That was rhetorical question, wasn't it?" I ask.

He brushes a stray hair from my face and tucks it behind my ear. "Maybe. Then again, maybe not."

He leans down and I know he's going to kiss me. I should do it, if for no other reason than to give Matt a chance and prove to myself that I'm open to being with someone besides Caleb.

His lips meet mine and he wraps his arm around me. It's not passionate and hot like Caleb's kisses, but it's nice and safe and warm and...

I pull away. "I can't."

Matt looks sad. "Maybe we're not ready to move on after all."

My cell phone in my purse starts ringing. I don't know if Matt is right or wrong. I like Matt...I've always liked Matt. He's a great guy that any girl should be proud to date.

So why couldn't I kiss Matt without thinking about Caleb?

My phone rings again and I fish it out of my purse. It's probably my mom, since I'd left a message for her after I charged my phone in the suite. But when I look at the Caller ID, I feel a jolt of surprise. It's Leah Becker, Caleb's sister. We stopped being friends after the accident, but after Caleb left Paradise, we started talking again. Leah's emotions run high, and they're right on the surface. She's emotionally fragile and no longer the best friend I once knew. I hope she'll snap out of it at some point.

"Hey, Leah. I'm glad you called." I watch as Matt joins the rest of the group, giving me privacy.

"Hey, Maggie," Leah says softly. She's still got a lot of issues regarding the accident, and even though I've forgiven her, she hasn't actually forgiven herself. "How's the trip?"

"Good. We've only talked to one group so far, but it was okay. Right now we're staying at the dorms at Freeman University, right by the Wisconsin border. What have you been doing?"

Silence. Leah doesn't talk as much as she used to, so I pretty much hold up our conversations now. It's okay. I know it's part of her own healing process.

"Not much," she finally says. "Just hanging around, mostly."

That's pretty much all there is to do in Paradise in the summer. Some people take vacations, but most people stay in Paradise and never leave. I know two people who left Paradise—my father and Caleb.

That thought freezes me in my tracks, and I just stand on the sidewalk as the rest of the groups walks ahead of me. I stare blindly after them while the reality hits me: I get left behind by the men in my life who are supposed to love me.

I blink, and focus on the restaurant a half a block away. Everyone is out front, gesturing for me to get off the phone. I can't hang up with Leah without telling her, "Caleb's here."

"W-w-what do you mean?" she asks nervously.

"He's on the trip."

"With you?"

"Yeah."

"Why? How? Where has he been? Is he okay?" she asks, panic laced in her voice. "Okay, that's so weird. I really called you because I wanted to talk about Caleb and I didn't know who else to call besides you. How did you end up on the same trip as my brother?

"I don't know how it happened, exactly. I think he's been living in Chicago since he left town. He's changed, though. He's not the same." I don't tell her my goal is to get Caleb back to Paradise to work things out. Leah needs him. His family needs him. I thought I needed him, but now we're too different. I can't be emotionally involved with someone who resents the world and wants to push everyone away.

I hear hesitation in Leah's voice as she says, "I always used to think an ESP thing between twins was something people made up. But I couldn't sleep the past few nights, Maggie. I swear Caleb is in trouble, or *really* unhappy. I feel his pain as if it's my own. That's stupid, isn't it?"

"No, it's not stupid," I tell her. I believe anything is possible. It's probably because I'm an over-emotional person. It's one of my flaws.

"Do me a favor, will you?"

"What is it?" I ask.

"Take care of him, Maggie. Promise me you'll watch out for my brother," she says almost desperately.

Watch out for him? Caleb is strong enough, if not emotionally than definitely physically, to take care of himself.

"Don't worry, Leah," I tell her. I swallow a lump in my throat and temporarily push away my newfound resolve to let go of Caleb once and for all. "I'll make sure he stays out of trouble."

ELEVEN

Caleb

"**Y**ou're a great dancer," Brandi says as we walk outside after we unload a beer bong in the kitchen. This girl is no stranger to beer bongs, I'll tell you that much. She's a damn pro.

I mumble, "Thanks."

She holds on to my elbow to steady herself and looks up at me with big brown eyes. "You know what they say about good dancers, don't you?"

Sure I know, but I want to hear the explanation come through Brandi's little lips … so I've got to ask. "What do they say?"

She gives me a wicked smile and giggles. "Good dancers are good in bed."

Brandi's words make me feel like a rock star. She definitely feeds my bruised ego.

"Wanna test that theory?" I ask. Okay, I'm officially drunk.

She bites her bottom lip, assessing me like a car. I wonder if she thinks I'm a Chevy or a Rolls Royce. She leans in and whispers in my ear, "I'm a good dancer, too."

I pull this sexy girl close. Her arms wrap around my neck and she presses against me. It's a hint of more to come. I'm gonna let myself enjoy Brandi. She's a surefire solution to this pity party I've been throwing myself for way too long. No doubt she's gonna make me forget about Maggie and everything else.

I don't know how much alcohol I have in my system, but it's enough to make my head swim and make me believe the only girl I'm interested in is the one pressing her hot body against mine, which is good. Very good.

"Let's go to your place," I tell her. I don't think Maggie or Damon would be too appreciative if they came back and caught me gettin' it on with a girl. And if Lenny found us ... hell, the guy might be demented enough to ask to join in the fun.

She leads me down the quad, tripping a couple of times. I steady her and she calls me her hero. Yeah, right We stagger past the place I played football earlier, but she stops when we get to Dixon Hall.

"You live *here*?" I ask her as I fight the sobering thought that we might get caught by the Re-START posse.

"Yeah. Don't worry, though. My roommate is out for the night."

She leads me up the stairs to the second floor. Damn. Her room is just down the hall from ours. Brandi doesn't have a suite like the one I'm in—hers is just a small dorm room with two single beds.

I watch with lazy eyes as she stumbles over to the bed and unbuttons her shirt. She watches me with raised eyebrows as she pushes the material aside like curtains being opened to let in the daylight sun, revealing a lacy black bra that doesn't hide much. I like easy girls who don't expect me to be one of the good guys. If they wear lacy black bras, all the better. I whip my shirt off and walk toward her.

"Your tattoo is so sexy," she purrs as we lie on the bed together. "It's like black fire." I got my tattoo in Chicago as a symbol of my rebellion.

Being here with Brandi is a symbol of my rebellion, too.

We haven't kissed yet. I'm not sure I even want to kiss her. And while that thought should be alarming me, I don't think about it too hard because (1) it's damn difficult to think straight when you're drunk, and (2) she maneuvers around to straddle me and my mind goes blank.

She traces the tattoo on my biceps with her fingers. "Wanna see mine?"

"Sure."

She kneels above me, turns around, and pulls down the back of her pants. Sure enough, she's got a tattoo of a red unicorn with rainbow wings right above her ass crack.

"Nice," I say, but I'm starting to feel anxious so I add, "Show me what else you've got." We'd better get this party started because I should go back to my own room soon. I better not be missing when Damon and the rest of the crew comes back.

Brandi licks her heart-shaped lips as she twists back around and unbuttons her low-slung pants. "I like a guy who knows what he wants. What do you want, Caleb?"

"I'm up for anything and everything."

"Me too," she says, raking her nails down my chest and moving lower. And lower. It hurts, and I think she's scratching off a layer or two of my skin. She slithers down my body, and I decide I don't care.

I lie back, welcoming what I know will come next. As her expert hands unsnap and unzip my jeans, then free me from confinement, I watch, my head spinning. She's having no problem focusing, even though she's as wasted as me. Everything she does is so well orchestrated; this girl is a total pro at more than just beer bongs. I close my eyes and tell my lower region to enjoy the attention.

I am definitely into this.

Way into this.

To say I'm turned on right now is an understatement of mega proportions. I'm just not sure if it's a problem that behind my eyelids I'm imagining a girl who limps and hates me...

Maggie.

"What did you just say?"

Huh? "What?" I open my eyes and look down at Brandi, poised above my unzipped pants.

"Did you just call me Maggie?" she asks accusingly.

"No." Whether I did or didn't, Brandi is *definitely* not Maggie. "Sorry," I add lamely.

She shrugs. "That's okay."

Without hesitation, she reaches into her side table drawer and pulls out a little plastic bag. She picks out a yellow pill with a smiley face on it, pops it in her mouth, and breathes in slowly as she savors the taste. "Here, take an Adam," she says, holding another one out to me.

I look at the pill. "What's an Adam?"

"You know, Ecstasy. Take it and put it under your tongue. I promise you won't think about anything else but having a good time with me."

Sounds great. I sit up and take the pill from her. If taking this little thing can make me forget everything except having a good time, I'm all for it.

But as I'm about to pop it into my mouth, I think about my mom. My mom is a prescription drug addict. Getting shitfaced drunk is bad enough, but taking pills...

Fuck.

Ingesting pills takes this thing to an entirely different level. I hand the pill back to her. "I can't do this."

"Do what?" she asks hesitantly.

I move out from under her and pull up my jeans. "I don't know. I need a minute."

"For what?" she asks, now completely confused.

Good question. I look Brandi up and down. She's totally got it goin' on. She's beautiful and has a rockin' bod...but she's not Maggie. And while I don't want Maggie, or can't have Maggie, or whatever the hell it is that I can't put into a coherent thought because I'm drunk, this isn't gonna work unless I can pull it together.

"Where's the bathroom?" I ask.

"Down the hall. You okay? If you're thinking about buying protection out of the bathroom dispensers, you don't have to worry. I've got some."

I head out the door and mumble, "I'll be right back."

I stumble over to the guys' bathroom and lean over one of the sinks. This sucks. I should be enjoying my night off. Instead, I'm a moody drunk. I look into the mirror in front of me, and it makes me feel worse. I run my hand through my messed-up hair and wonder if I should shave it all off like they did in juvie, 'cause right now I'm not just a moody drunk...I'm a moody drunk who looks like shit.

What's worse is I feel as bad as I look.

I splash water on my face to help bring me out of this mood, but it's no use. Brandi was turning me on, but it wasn't Brandi making me hard. It was thoughts of Maggie. Twisted, I know. There's no way I can go through with this thing with a girl who's just a stand-in.

I head back toward her room. She's probably tripping by now and ready for some serious action. I hope she's not too pissed I'm skipping out on her XTC party early.

In the hallway, just as I've got my hand on Brandi's

doorknob, I hear Maggie's voice from behind me say, "That's not our suite, Caleb."

I look toward the girl who's been haunting my nights ever since I was locked up in jail. The girl who just ruined my sexual escapade with Brandi without even knowing it. She's got hazel eyes that change with her mood, so different from the girl I was lying in bed with a few minutes ago. And while Maggie looks damn hot to me, I doubt she has any unicorn tats above her ass or wears lacy black bras. I'd like to find out, though.

"I know," I say.

Maggie limps over to me, her eyebrows furrowed in confusion. "Then what are you doing out in the hall without a shirt on?" She looks me up and down. "And why are your, um, pants unbuttoned...and unzipped?"

The door to Brandi's room opens and Brandi appears. Her hair is mussed, her pants are undone and hanging loosely on her hips, and she's got her shirt clenched against the front of her bra. I'm screwed.

"Oh," Maggie mumbles, obviously getting her answer without me having to say a word.

"There you are," Brandi says with a smile, then looks over at Maggie. "Who are you?"

"His *girlfriend*," Maggie answers with a stern, straight face.

Brandi looks from Maggie to me, then back to Maggie. "You're kidding, right?"

TWELVE

Maggie

The girl with her barely there shirt clutched in front of her is waiting for an answer. Obviously she doesn't believe that a girl who looks like me could be dating a boy who looks like Caleb.

My insides clench in disgust. Caleb isn't my boyfriend and technically never was, but it still hurts to see him standing here in the hallway, his shirt off and pants unzipped, obviously ready to get it on with this girl.

I don't wait for him to tell the girl that the last person on earth he'd call his girlfriend would be me. Whether it hurts or not, I promised Leah that I would look after Caleb. She senses he's in trouble. Leah's twin-ESP senses were right on.

I skipped the movie tonight after the youth group dinner because I was tired and my leg started to ache. Little did I know I'd find Caleb here, like this, with another girl.

Looking at them together is a slap in the face. The girl he'd obviously already spent time with tonight is really pretty. She's got big brown eyes, perfect blonde hair, and a waist so small it's a wonder all her internal organs can fit inside her body. Maybe they're all stuffed into her huge boobs instead.

"No, I'm *not* kidding," I tell her, finding my voice again. "Caleb, come back to our suite."

He looks confused.

"Your shirt is still in my room," the girl says with a big grin. She probably expects him to blow me off, and she's probably right.

To my surprise, Caleb slings an arm over my shoulder. He smells like beer. "I gotta go with her."

I can detect a slight slur in his speech, confirming that he's not completely sober.

The girl ducks back in her room, but reappears a second later. She whips his shirt at him. "You're a loser," she says, and then looks at me. "You can have him."

When she slams the door, it's just Caleb and me standing in the hall. I shrug off his arm. He hasn't put his shirt back on and his zipper is still undone.

"Are you coming?" I ask impatiently.

I'm kind of surprised that he follows me back to our suite. I unlock the door.

"I need help," Caleb slurs as he drapes his arm across my shoulders again. I can feel the heat of his bare skin through my clothes. In the past I would have done anything for Caleb to put his arm around me. But not now.

"You have beer breath," I tell him, pushing him off me. "And if you want help zipping up your fly, you've asked the wrong girl."

He stumbles into the suite behind me and collapses on the couch. "So you're the wrong girl for me but the right girl for Matt?" he asks.

"Shut up, Caleb. Matt's just a friend."

"I don't think so. I think you've moved on to him."

"My relationships are none of your business. And just because I talk to a guy doesn't mean I've moved on to him."

"Right. I knew that." He looks around, confused. "Wait, where's the rest of our little dysfunctional group?"

"At a movie."

"Why aren't you with 'em?"

As if on cue, a sharp pain starts at my ankle and shoots up my calf. I would suck in a breath, but I don't want Caleb feeling sorry for me. "I need to rest my leg."

He pats the cushion next to him. "Take a load off and sit next to me."

Caleb's hair is sticking up in all different directions and that damn zipper is still open as a reminder of what he was doing with that girl tonight. Problem is, he still looks good. My top lip curls, thinking about him and that other girl. "No."

"Come on, just for a second."

His eyes are at half-mast and he's attempting to act all vulnerable and innocent, but I know better.

"You should probably go to bed before Damon catches you drunk or on drugs or whatever you ingested tonight," I tell him.

"Sit with me for a minute, then I'll disappear into my room and you won't have to see me for the rest of the night. I promise." He fumbles with his fly and finally zips and buttons his pants, then leans his head against the back of the couch. "And just so you know, I didn't do drugs. Could've, but didn't. Don't want to end up like my mom," he mumbles.

That's the first time I've heard him talk about his family since this trip started. I hear a distinct sadness in his voice when he mentions his mom, which makes him seem even more vulnerable.

I stand right in front of him, determined to be the rational one. "You were drinking tonight. Don't deny it."

His lips curve into a small smile. "Yeah, I drank. Feels good to not have to think about ... everything."

I hesitate. Being close to Caleb isn't a good idea. "I should report you to Damon."

"Yeah, you should."

I sigh. "But I won't."

"Why not, Mags? Could it be that deep down in that frozen heart of yours you still like me?"

He reaches out and pulls me toward him. Not being very steady in the first place, I stumble forward, but he cradles my body with his arm and gently lowers me to the couch until I'm lying down. Under him.

"Don't answer that question," he says.

My brain tells me to scramble away and keep my distance, but my body isn't listening to my brain. My body has a mind of its own. I look up into Caleb's intense, sea blue eyes. Those depths are totally focused on my lips, reminding me of the first time we kissed back in Paradise. It was at Paradise Park, right after he held me while I cried in his arms.

I swear the air grows thicker around us, closing in like a dark cloud. All I hear is the sound of our breathing. I forget everything else and let myself enjoy being this close to him again.

He brushes my hair away from my face with unexpected gentleness, the pads of his fingers a soft caress brushing across my cheek. I bunch my hands at my sides, afraid that if I actually move I'll slip back into reality.

Caleb shifts and moves closer. "Maggie, do you want this as much as I do?" he asks, his face poised right above mine.

"I ... I can't answer that."

He leans back just the slightest bit, but he's still close enough I can smell the alcohol he drank tonight.

"Why not?" he asks.

I move my hand to his bare chest to stop him before

I lose all common sense. Having him this close makes me breathe harder and my pulse race, which just makes me even angrier with myself than with him.

"Do you really have to ask? You were obviously with another girl tonight, Caleb. I'm not degrading myself by being sloppy seconds."

"I didn't kiss her. I swear."

When I give him an I-don't-believe-you look, his expression turns gravely serious. "I'm not gonna say we didn't fool around, but I couldn't go through with it 'cause I was…" He squeezes his eyes shut. After a second he opens his eyes and stares right into mine with that serious look again. "Forget it."

"Just go to bed," I tell him, trying to push him off of me. "It's obvious you're drunk and aren't thinking straight."

"Kiss me, then I'll go to bed."

"You're crazy," I choke.

"Yeah, I know." His lips are twisted into a half smile. "But humor me just this once." His head slowly dips toward mine. I watch and hold my breath as his beautiful, full lips get closer and closer. "Oh Maggie," he murmurs softly when I instinctively wrap my arms around his neck. "I need this."

I must not be thinking clearly, because I say against his lips, "Me too."

His hands are braced on either side of my head as he brushes his lips over mine. We kiss tentatively, as if we're both not sure it's okay. My heart is slowly melting. My entire body tingles with excitement and anticipation as one of his hands grabs my waist and pulls me closer.

I close my eyes and pretend we're back in Mrs. Reynolds' gazebo when it was just the two of us. It felt so good; it couldn't have been wrong. Back then he held me and made me believe that as long as we were together, everything else would fall into place.

I sigh into Caleb's open mouth; it comes out as a little whimper. He leans away from me. I open my eyes and find him smiling—a one-hundred-percent-satisfied male smile.

As if my response is his cue to take this further, Caleb gives a guttural growl right before he lowers his head again. His mouth is on mine, open, his tongue searching. I think my brain is trying to send off warning signals, but my body and my own tongue are enjoying the attention too much to listen. The sounds of our tongues and lips and moans spur me on, and I find myself raking my hands through his hair, pulling him closer.

"Touch me," Caleb urges as he reaches out and traces my lips with the soft tip of his finger and dips it into my mouth.

I convince myself to think of the gazebo. As long as I keep my eyes closed, we're there—we're in the past and not the present. He's going to tell me how much he cares about me any minute now. He's going to tell me that I'm the only girl he wants and needs.

He traces a wet path down my neck and dips his finger into my the V of my T-shirt. His mouth follows with little kisses before he moves up and kisses me again. I start to sweat with passion. I'm on fire.

It's all slow and erotic, our tongues reaching out and gliding and searching as if we're both savoring the taste of each other. The bitter taste of beer has been replaced by this sweet scent that reminds me solely of Caleb. I'm lost in the present, but my mind and body are stuck in the past. It feels good and oh, so right to be finally kissing him like this. And touching him.

He said he needs this.

I wasn't lying when I admitted I needed it, too.

When he reaches under my shirt and rubs his thumb across the top of my bra, the rest of his hand cradling my breast, I feel like the world has stopped and it's just the two of us left. I feel a warm sensation running from my breast to the tips of my toes and back again. My insides are slowly melting into little puddles.

Until my cell phone rings. It's in my purse, ringing loudly and interrupting my fantasy.

"Don't answer it," Caleb rasps. "Ignore it."

He kisses me again, but the gazebo is gone. The moment is lost.

My cell phone keeps ringing. I turn my head, breaking the kiss, and blink a sudden tear of frustration away as I send my arm flailing for my purse.

"I can't." My hand finds the side pocket and I grab my cell. The number glowing on the Caller ID makes me suck in a breath. "It's my dad," I say slowly as I nudge Caleb's hand away from under my shirt. I let the phone ring and ring until the call gets transferred to voicemail.

My dad, the guy who calls me once or twice a year. My dad, who left me and barely looks back.

I look up at Caleb, still poised above me. He's the boy who left and didn't look back until we were forced together on this trip. He betrayed me just like my dad did. He lied to me just like my dad did.

He fooled around with another girl tonight, then moved on to me like it didn't matter. Different face, different body, same interchangeable good time.

I'm pathetic and the only one I can blame is me. I could have said no. I could have acted like I didn't want this. I could have walked into my bedroom and shut the door.

But I didn't.

Instead, I stepped closer to him … almost testing him to see if he'd make a move. Sure enough, he took the bait. I'm no better than that girl he was with tonight.

"Caleb, what are we doing?" I ask.

He leans away from me to sit up again and sighs. "Oh, no, here it comes. Your introspective, emotional, and philosophical self is coming out."

"Why shouldn't I be introspective? *We* don't make sense."

"Neither does chocolate and peanut butter, but somehow it works," he says. "Somehow the mixture of those two things is genius."

"You're drunk. I'm not talking about food. I'm talking about two people with a really screwed-up past—"

"Stop thinking so much," he says, finishing my sentence. "No matter how much time has passed, it doesn't seem to matter." He rubs my arm gently, tickling my sensitive skin. "I don't know why we're both fighting it so much. Hell, I couldn't do it with Brandi tonight because all I could think about was you. I even called her your name," he says, rambling. "Yeah, it's screwed up, we're screwed up, but why hide the fact that we still want each other?"

I push him away. "You, Caleb Becker, are one big jerk."

"I don't get you," he says, his hands in the air and his eyebrows furrowed in confusion. "I admitted I couldn't be with another girl because I was thinking of you. I want you, Maggie. Is that so wrong?"

"Yes."

"What, admitting you turn me on? Why are you treating it as if it's an insult?"

"I don't want us to just 'want' each other." I take a deep breath. "I want a real relationship with a guy. Love. And you, you don't even know what love is. Love is *honesty*. Love is a *mutual respect* for one another, something you and I don't have."

"Oh, really?" My words obviously make him pissed, because he stands up and fires back, "So you're saying you have no respect for me?"

"Yeah, that's what I'm saying."

"Fine," he says.

"Fine," I say.

"I guess I pegged this thing going on between us all wrong, then."

This time the sharp pain strikes my heart, but I stay strong. "It's all about honesty, Caleb."

"Yeah, well, *honestly* you're being ridiculous."

THIRTEEN

Caleb

I'm lying in bed staring at the ceiling. Lenny and Matt are asleep. I haven't talked to or heard from Maggie since we both stormed to our rooms four hours ago.

I told her I still want her. Admitted that I never stopped wanting her. And she goes and starts talking about love. Fucking love. And honesty.

Love isn't about honesty. It's about protecting the people you love from things that will hurt them. That's love.

Oh, hell. I told Maggie I still want her and we should give in to our lust for each other. Stupid, I know. I didn't mean to blurt it out then and there—it just happened. Maybe it was the beer. Yeah, right. I'm still buzzed, but I knew what I was doing. Doesn't make it any less stupid, though.

For the next week, Maggie practically ignores me. We travel each day to some event where Damon introduces us and urges us to share our sob stories. All of us share. My story is the shortest. "I drove drunk and hit a girl. Went to jail for it. I was practically kicked out of my parents' house and lost my girlfriend. I got my license suspended for three years and I'm pretty much living on the streets now. So, um, don't drink and drive."

Yep, that's my story and I'm sticking to it.

It's not until we're on a panel at some random high school auditorium sitting behind a table when I get asked a question I'm not sure how to answer.

It comes out of the mouth of a fifteen-year-old kid in a summer school driver's ed class. "This question is for the guy in the blue T-shirt on the end," he says.

I look at everyone else. Unfortunately nobody but me is wearing a blue shirt. Erin passes the microphone to me. "What's your question?" I ask lazily, my voice echoing through the auditorium.

"Why did your parents kick you out?"

Shit, do I really have to answer that? My sister refused to tell the truth about the accident, my mom is addicted to prescription drugs, and my dad is in denial. "That's a good question," I say, stalling. I don't know what to say. The truth and the lies are starting to melt together as I clear my throat and think of how to answer. "My parents were embarrassed to have an ex-con as a kid. On top of that, they weren't too keen on the fact that I was fooling around with the girl I went to jail for hitting with my car."

"Why'd you do that?" the kid asks. "I mean, why fool around with the girl you hit? Wasn't that a bad idea?"

"Yeah. It was a really bad idea. One of the stupidest ideas I've ever had. Next question?"

The next question is for Lenny. They want to know why he drove a car into the lake.

"It seemed like a good idea at the time," Lenny says. "Of course I was drunk, but that's no excuse. I paid a big price and I wish I could do it over."

That seems to be the theme of our lives . . . wishing we could turn back time and make different choices.

During the van drive back to Freeman, Maggie won't even look in my direction. She sits next to Matt and chats with him about tennis. When we're back at our dorm, she heads straight for her room. Damon heads for his room, too. When his door closes and the rest of the group is in the lounge area, I step into Maggie's room.

"What's your problem?" I ask softly so the rest of the group can't hear.

"I don't want to talk about it," she says, then starts to move away from me.

I grab her wrist and tug gently, urging her to face me.

"Get your hand off her," Matt says from behind me.

I glare at the guy who obviously wants Maggie to be more than a friend. "What are you, her bodyguard?"

"Maybe." Matt steps between me and Maggie.

"Don't get in the middle of this, man." I'm all tense because, well, once I was Maggie's protector against this asshole Vic Medonia, and now Matt's making me feel like I'm no better than Vic.

"She obviously doesn't want to talk to you right now."

When I look over at Maggie, she's pointing toward the door for me to get out.

"I'm done," I tell her.

In the morning, when Damon shakes me awake, I tell him I'm taking the day off.

"Caleb, get your butt up. You're not getting out of today's activities, so don't even think about it," Damon says.

"I'm sick," I say.

"With what?"

"Annoyance. Seriously, Damon, Lenny's cell phone went off every couple of hours last night."

"He's telling the truth," Matt says as he pulls a tank over his head. "We kept telling him to turn the damn thing off, but he wouldn't."

"I turned it to vibrate!" Lenny calls out from the lounge.

Matt walks to the door and yells out, "Having it vibrate on the desk is as bad as having it ring, dude."

Damon leans down and pulls the covers off me. "I'll confiscate Lenny's phone tonight, but you're still joining us today, Caleb. I have a special activity planned. No excuses."

I drag myself out of bed, shower, and get dressed. I think Maggie has the girls on her side, because they're all ignoring me today. Even during breakfast, Trish offers everyone a blueberry muffin except for me and Lenny. How I got to be lumped in the same category as a fucking tool like Lenny is beyond me. On the other hand, Saint Matt is treated like a damn king. Not only does he get a muffin, but Maggie actually pours him a glass of orange juice from the small fridge. And smiles at him as she places the glass in front of him.

I'm even more annoyed now.

After breakfast, we all pile into the van. I'm stuck sitting in the very back with Lenny, who doesn't seem to mind or care that the girls are ignoring him. Or maybe the guy is just used to people ignoring him, or is too stupid to realize it.

Damon pulls up to a wooded property with a big sign that reads *VICTORY BOUND—BUILDING STRONG FOUNDATIONS IS THE KEY TO SUCCESS.*

"Is this a Habitat for Humanity project?" I ask. To be honest, I wouldn't mind getting a hammer and nails in my hands. I used to work construction for my uncle during the summers. Getting my frustration out on a nail and a two-by-four sounds like a sweet idea right about now.

"No, it's nothing like that," Damon says, to my disappointment.

We pile out of the van and Damon tells us we're having a meeting. "This is a skill-building camp. I've noticed that many of you have issues with asking people for help and trusting others."

"Maybe we like it that way," I murmur.

"Not a good way to live, Caleb. It's human nature to need people and to live in harmony with others. You need this...and I'm not just talking about Caleb." He points to everyone else in the group. "You *all* need this."

A guy comes out of the door marked *Office*. He looks like a mountain man or Bigfoot come to life, complete with a long beard and unruly hair. "You must be the Re-START group." He holds out his hand to Damon and they shake. "I'm Dex, the owner of Victory Bound."

The first thing Dex does is have us stand in a circle under some trees. He instructs us to say one word that describes ourselves.

Matt says, "Loyal."

Lenny says, "Funny."

Erin says, "Sad."

Trish says, "Angry."

Maggie says, "Confused."

I don't miss the fact that she's looking directly at me when she says it. Is she confused about *us*? That's news to me. Maggie pretty much shuts me down every time we get close. She doesn't seem confused at all.

When it's my turn, I say, "Screwed up" because that pretty much sums up who and what I am.

"That doesn't count," Lenny says. "Dex said to say *one*

word that describes you. 'Screwed up' is technically two words."

"And 'shut up before I kick the shit out of you' is ten words," I say in a warning tone.

Dex/Bigfoot holds his hand up. "No threatening your teammates, Caleb. Victory Bound rules. Apologize," he orders.

Apologize? Is this guy serious? I'd rather eat broken glass then apologize to Lenny.

Damon the Enforcer gives me a level stare. "Come on, Caleb. Spit it out so we can move on."

"Yeah," Trish says, then snorts. "Don't be such a jerk."

I look over at Maggie. "Just do it," she mouths silently.

"Nope." I used to play by the rules, but I haven't done it for so long I've forgotten how.

"Channel your energy into positive actions," Dex says to me.

I stick my hands in my pockets and face Dex. "What if I don't feel positive?"

"*Doing* something positive will help turn your mood around. When you smile, your body relaxes. When you experience positive human touch and interaction, it eases tension in your body."

The last time I had positive human touch was with Maggie when she kissed me and touched me on the couch in our suite. It felt amazing until she pushed me away.

"I want to see you two hug," Dex says.

"You're kiddin' me, right?"

"I'm not kidding. I think you should hug Lenny."

I don't move my hands out of my pockets. "Yeah, umm, I don't think so." I want to say *no fucking way* to Bigfoot, but hold back.

Lenny opens his arms out wide and smiles at me. "Come to Papa."

"Come on, Caleb," Damon urges. "Just try it."

"I'd rather hug one of the girls, Damon. Or Matt, for that matter."

Nobody seems to care about listening to the list of things I'd rather do than hug Lenny. They're all just waiting for me to cave.

Lenny steps forward, his arms still open.

I step out of the circle, an obvious outsider. Bigfoot doesn't seem pleased. "It's not about the hug…it's about your character. Doing something you don't want to do to please someone else is an act of kindness."

I give a short laugh. "Listen, Dex, I'm being kind by warning Lenny before I kick his ass. Give me some credit. Shit, man. I hung out with gang members in Chicago who thought kindness was asking what limb you wanted cut off before they chopped you into pieces and fed you to dogs."

"Do you want to be a part of this group, or not?" Bigfoot asks, ignoring my gang scenario.

"Not."

"He has no choice," Damon bellows loudly. "He's part of this group whether he likes it or not. Right, Caleb?"

"Right," I say. Unless I ditch them all and take my chances. But I won't, because if juvie sucked, I've got a feeling the big-time jail will put me over the edge. I step back into the circle.

"We can hug later," Lenny says to me.

I shake my head. "Don't count on it."

I'm definitely on Dex's shit list, that's for sure. He shoots me these looks probably designed to make me feel bad, but they don't. After what happened with Maggie, I'm done with feeling remorse.

Dex tells us we'll be expected to complete a bunch of Victory Bound tasks that have us working together as a team. The first task is a puzzle we have to complete while three of us instruct three blindfolded members of our group on how to organize the pieces. The next task is a maze we have to wind through while attached to each other with rope. Then we have to build a race car using items found in nature. Maggie doesn't look my way the entire time.

After lunch, Dex leads our group into the woods behind the main office. He stops when we get to a thick oak tree with a small platform nailed to the trunk about a foot off the ground.

"This is a trust exercise," Dex explains. "I'll split you up into pairs. Each of you will turn your back to your partner while standing up on the platform, then fall into your partner's arms. Then we'll switch who falls and who catches."

He pairs Lenny and Trish, then Matt and Erin, then

me and Maggie. I stand next to my frowning partner. "Don't look so depressed," I tell her.

"I'm not depressed. Didn't you hear him say this was a trust exercise?"

"Yeah, so?"

She shakes her head. "Forget it."

Before I can respond, Trish cries out, "Lenny will flatten me! I hope you have medical insurance, Dex."

Lenny laughs. "You're not a lightweight yourself, Trish. If I drop you, will your boobs burst when they hit the ground?"

Dex holds up his hand, which we've all learned by now is his special signal for "shut up." "You can all do this, I assure you. You'll be attached by a bungee cord secured to the tree, which will lessen the weight load. Lenny and Trish, you two go first."

"No, way, Dex," Trish says. "What if he drops me?"

"He won't."

"How can you be so sure?"

"Because the entire group is counting on him, and he won't let us down. Right, Lenny?"

Lenny's eyebrows are furrowed in confusion. "Is that some psychobabble bullshit you're using on me?"

"Yes. Now stand on the platform and attach the bungee around your waist. Show Trish how easy it is."

Lenny does as Dex instructs. With the bungee taking the brunt of the weight, Trish has no problem catching him. They switch places, and to our relief Lenny catches Trish and doesn't test his theory about her boobs.

"Okay," Dex says, moving on. "Caleb and Maggie, you're up."

FOURTEEN

Maggie

I step to the edge of the platform, hook the bungee cord attached to the tree around my waist, and look down. Caleb is standing there with his arms out, ready to catch me.

Suddenly, somehow, this exercise goes beyond whether I believe he'll catch me or not.

That's why I've been so angry with him since that night last week... the thought brings me up short. I haven't been mad at him since just that night. I've been mad at him for eight months. Since I found out he lied. Since he left without telling me the truth.

I think of all the things left unsaid... all the things I should have said. There's so much dishonesty between us.

I back myself against the tree and wrap my arms around myself. "I can't."

"Why not?" Caleb asks.

Everyone is staring at me, waiting for an explanation. And while I don't want to talk about this in front of the group, I'm so tired of the secrets. I desperately want to say what I'm feeling right here and now because I might just lose the nerve to say it later.

I unhook the bungee cord and step off. "I just don't want to do it."

"I'm not gonna let you fall," Caleb says. "I promise."

I look into his piercing blue eyes, which get darker when he's upset.

"It's not about whether you're going to catch me or not," I tell him. "It's about the accident."

Caleb looks wary and confused, and I'm pretty sure his mood is about to get even worse when I tell him, "This whole exercise is about trust. The truth is, I don't trust you."

"This is gettin' good," Lenny says, rubbing his hands together. "And all along I thought you two were gettin' it on while nobody was watchin'."

Caleb shoots the guy a glare. "Shut your mouth for once, Lenny, or I'll shut it for you." His hands are now in tight fists at his side and the muscle in his jaw is twitching. I think he's ready to take Lenny on, but this isn't about Lenny. It's about us.

Dex holds a hand up, but I don't think Caleb cares.

"After all we've been through, I think you owe me trust," Caleb says to me.

He doesn't get it. Oh, how I want him to tell me the truth about the accident on his own. It's the only way we can move past this. I *need* to move past the lies and deceit.

Thinking about the accident and all that's happened since makes my body shiver. I'll never be the same physically. I'll always be looked at as a cripple. I wanted to believe Caleb wanted me despite my injuries, but maybe it was just a tactic to encourage me to keep my mouth shut.

The only person who can bring the truth out in the open is standing here with me now.

"Face the cold, hard facts, Caleb. You don't trust me, either." I can't stop now. Tears roll down my face as I walk right up to Caleb and jab my finger at his chest. "You lied to me! You deceived me! The least you could do after we started getting close was be honest."

He stares at me, his eyebrows drawn tight over his confused eyes.

"Tell me the truth about the accident, Caleb. I *dare* you."

I see the moment he gets it and stiffens, shocked.

Caleb shakes his head and steps away from me. "Don't do this."

"Tell everyone here what really happened that night." I open my arms wide and look up at the sky. "Scream it out loud and set us all free from the lies!"

Lenny holds his hands up as if he's in church. "Hal-lelujah!"

Caleb rushes Lenny, and tackles him. And punches him. Lenny punches back. I'm scared, and I'm screaming for them to stop wrestling, especially because Caleb is a trained wrestler and Lenny doesn't stand a chance against him. In an instant, Damon pulls Caleb off Lenny and starts yelling for Caleb to calm down. Caleb is in a rage now, and I'm not sure he can hear anything though his anger.

"Caleb, get a hold of yourself," Damon orders.

Caleb breaks free of Damon's hold. His hands are in fists, ready to fight. "No!"

"This isn't about Lenny!" I yell, trying to get his attention. "It's about you and me."

Caleb looks at me. His breathing is ragged and his eyes look intense and fierce. He's not ready to back down, not by a long shot.

"I'm the one who got hit by that car, not you," I tell him. "Don't act like you're the victim here. You made choices I didn't ask you to make. I'm not sure anyone asked you to make them." I'm screaming the words, not caring that the entire world can probably hear me. "You think I like limping everywhere I go? I don't. I'm the victim! Be honest with me! You didn't care about me enough to trust me. I gave you my heart, but it wasn't enough." I start to walk away, the leaves crunching hard beneath my shoes.

"Let's get one thing straight, sweetheart," he says from behind me. "I *never* asked you to be my girlfriend."

I stop and turn back to him. "No, you didn't ask. But you sure did everything in your power to make us a couple. You kissed me by the tree in Paradise Park. You were the one who told me at Mrs. Reynolds' house that you wanted to be where I was. You were the one who..." My throat feels like there's a lump the size of a baseball inside. "You said what we had was real, but it was all a lie. Admit it."

"What do you want me to say, Maggie?"

"The truth! That's all I've ever wanted."

"I can't."

"*Can't* or *won't?*"

"What's the difference at this point?"

I swipe my eyes with the back of my hand because tears are blurring my vision. I don't care at all about our stunned audience. "You're nothing but a coward! Every guy in my life has disappointed me. First my dad, now you."

He looks at me like I'm the enemy. "I'm nothing like your dad. Don't insult me by putting us in the same sentence."

I give a short laugh. "He left me. You left me. He betrayed me by leaving and never turning back to see if I was okay. You betrayed me by leaving and never turning back to see if I was okay. He lies to me. You lie to me. You're *exactly* like him."

"You have no fucking clue, Maggie."

I continue limping away, heading for the office, or the van, or... I don't know where I'm headed except that I know I need to get away. Maybe if I put some space between Caleb and me this crushing pain in my heart will subside.

"Lies are easier to swallow than the truth, Maggie," Caleb yells. He doesn't follow me this time.

I stop but I don't turn around. "You're wrong."

"The *truth* is that I didn't want to have anything to do with you when I got released from jail and came back to Paradise. I *blamed* you for being the reason I went to jail. I *blamed* you for ruining my life. And even through all the blame and all the resentment, I fell for you. Your damn humming, your damn insecurity, your damn vulnerability...and that time you cried in my arms and held onto me like I was your pillar of strength, I was lost because I knew whatever was brewing between us was real. I hated myself for falling for you."

"So you left."

"What did you want me to do? We had to hide our relationship from your mother, my mom was on drugs, my dad was a damn doormat, and my sister...well, you saw her. She looked like death warmed over."

"If you just told the truth—"

"The truth sucks!" Caleb yells, anger and frustration dripping off his words.

"So you've decided to hide behind the lies, right?" Now I turn to face him across little patches of grass and dirt and leaves. I look him right in the eye. I'm not backing down.

Tense seconds tick by.

Caleb pounds his fist hard into the tree trunk. His knuckles are bleeding from the force, but he doesn't seem to notice as he storms up to me.

"The truth is that I didn't hit you with that car! I went to *fucking* jail for a whole *fucking* year for something I didn't *fucking* do! And you know what? It sucked. I resented every moment in juvie because I wasn't supposed to be there in the first place!"

His eyes go wide, his breathing is fast and furious. He turns around and focuses his attention on an outwardly shocked Damon, then scans the other members of our group, all of whom are equally shocked.

Caleb squeezes his eyes shut and winces, as if he wants to take back every truthful word he just spouted. When he opens his eyes, there's no emotion in them anymore. He's masked it.

"Happy now?" he growls.

FIFTEEN

Caleb

If my life wasn't complete shit before, it's definitely shit now. I just gave away the secret I promised to take to the grave. I betrayed my twin sister, and myself, all because I couldn't stand the way Maggie looked at me as she peered down from that damn platform. Her eyes were like glass, and the disappointed furrowing of her eyebrows made me want to scoop her up and take her to a place where nobody would deceive her or hurt her. A place where even I couldn't hurt her.

I fucked up. With Maggie, with Leah, with my parents...with everything.

At this point I can't even trust myself *not* to fuck up. What's the use in trying to stay out of jail when, maybe, that's the best place for me? At least in jail I know where I stand and don't have to see disappointment on the faces of the people I care about.

Problem is, I don't want to be locked up again. I felt like a restless, caged animal in juvie, especially because I knew I didn't deserve to be there in the first place. Or maybe I did. Maybe I deserved to be locked up for lying to the judge and everyone else. I was piss drunk the night Maggie got hit with the car, and maybe my judgment was off when I told my sister I would cover for her.

By then it was too late.

All I wanted to do was protect Leah, since I knew she wouldn't be able to handle the stress of being arrested and stuck in a cell. I don't even know what's right and wrong anymore.

How did Maggie know I'd lied to her? A second ago, I thought the only way I could take that betrayed look off her face was to tell her the truth. Another bad move. She already knew the truth.

I want to escape, but I'm stuck here. I might not be in a cage, but it feels like I'm in one.

"No, I'm not happy," Maggie finally says, her voice low and sad.

I glare at her. "Great, 'cause that makes two of us."

"Three of us," Lenny says, still on the ground. "I think I'm gonna have a bruise on my sensitive ass cheek from you tackling me."

Tears are falling down Maggie's cheeks. She blinks a

couple of times and swipes them away with her fingertips. "Do you hate me, Caleb?"

I should. I should hate her with all my soul, but I don't.

"You knew all along I didn't run into you, didn't you?" I say.

She nods. "I remembered bits and pieces like it was a puzzle, but it wasn't pieced together until—"

"Did you realize I wasn't the one who hit you before I left Paradise eight months ago?" I ask, needing to know the answer even though I'm dreading hearing it.

"Yes," she says softly.

I remember the times we spent together working at Mrs. Reynolds' house, when we fooled around in the gazebo and I ran my hands over her smooth, milky soft skin. "You knew I didn't hurt you, but you let me go along with thinking that you did. How could you?"

"By the time I realized who was really driving the car, I'd already forgiven you. It didn't matter."

"The hell it didn't matter!"

"Umm, time out. I think this activity is over," Damon says. "The three of us need to talk, like right now."

Now. That's Damon's favorite word.

The three of us leave the rest of the group at the platform with Dex and head for a picnic table by the parking lot.

Damon sighs as he looks at Maggie and me sitting opposite him. "Caleb, let me get this straight. You pled guilty to a crime you didn't commit?"

I look the guy straight in the eye. "I plead the fifth."

"You can't plead the fifth, Caleb," Damon says. "You're not in court."

Yeah, and I don't want to end up there again. "I'm still not answering the question."

Damon turns to Maggie for answers, since I'm obviously no help at all. "Maggie, what do you know about all this?"

Maggie shrugs.

Damon shakes his finger at both of us. "You give me no choice. If you won't explain, I'll have to reopen your file and investigate on my own."

"I went to jail, Damon," I blurt out. "I paid for the crime. Case closed."

"If you really went to jail for a crime you didn't commit, the case is far from over. Ever hear of taking responsibility for your actions? You think you did someone a favor? Guess again. If it wasn't you who hit Maggie, who was it?"

I stay silent while Damon looks to Maggie for answers. She stares at the ground.

"I warned you. This isn't over," he tells us.

We trudge through the rest of the exercises. I'm sure as hell not saying a word, and I'm freaking out wondering exactly how much Maggie knows.

After dinner, Damon pulls Maggie and me aside. "Tomorrow morning the rest of the group is going to another school for a panel talk, and the two of you are coming with me."

At the dorm, I overhear Damon talking a bunch of times on his cell, and I get the distinct feeling that he's about to have me arrested and interrogated.

I can't do this. The rest of the night is a big blur to me. All I can think about is that I have to get away. I have to ditch the group and head out on my own again.

In the middle of the night, when everyone is asleep, I toss everything I own in my duffle. Getting away from Damon and his ties to the Illinois justice system is the only solution. If they can't find me, Damon might not have a case against Leah. I looked at some legal books in the juvie library. The statute of limitations on a felony is three years. In a year, Leah can no longer be charged with the crime.

I leave our dorm suite and trot down the stairs. As I start across the dark campus, I hear a familiar voice behind me.

"Caleb, wait."

"Maggie, what are you doing?"

She's wearing silky pants and a T-shirt. Her hair is back in a ponytail, and she looks so vulnerable right now. And sexy, but she doesn't know it. Before I went to jail, I never gave her a second glance. She was just our neighbor and my twin sister's best friend. I was only interested in Kendra Greene, with her big hair and layers of makeup. Maggie's beauty is more subtle ... it can be missed if you're blinded by other girls, or compare her to them.

She bites her bottom lip. "You're leaving, aren't you?"

"I can't stay here." I toss my duffle over my shoulder and start walking again.

"I'm going with you," she calls out.

"No, you're not." I glance back at her. She's limping behind me with a backpack on her shoulders. "Go back to the dorm."

"No."

"Don't be stupid, Maggie. Go back to the group and move on with your life. Forget I ever existed."

"I can't do that," she says. "I wish the accident never happened, and that you hadn't gone to jail, and that you hadn't left Paradise, and that you didn't think getting involved with me was the biggest mistake of your life."

Shit. I hate having those words thrown back at me, especially when they were lies. I hurt her, even if I swore I'd never do it again. "Being with you wasn't a mistake."

She gazes up at me with those innocent, expressive eyes. "But you said—"

"Yeah, I know what I said. I lied. But you still can't come with me."

"You asked me to go with you the last time you left Paradise. Remember?"

I nod slowly.

"I'm not making that same mistake again. This time I'm coming with you."

SIXTEEN

Maggie

I can't let Caleb go. Not now. Not until I can convince him to go home again and make everything right. If I let him leave, I may never see him again. He disappeared without a trace eight months ago and I won't let that happen again. Not when everything is out in the open and there are no more lies between us.

"You don't have a choice," I tell him, putting my foot down.

He shakes his head. "Don't piss me off more than I already am."

He walks down the sidewalk that leads off campus. I follow. If he starts to jog, there's no way I can keep up with him.

"I didn't intend to piss you off," I tell him, matching his stride.

"Just ruin my life?"

"Me? I didn't ruin your life, Caleb. You've done that just fine on your own."

"Do me a favor. If you're so intent on joining me, keep the blabber to a minimum."

"You're crabby."

"Damn straight." He stops and turns to me. "Do you know what you did to me today? You made me give up information I promised to take to my grave. I feel like shit."

"If it makes you feel better, I feel like shit too. I don't want you to be pissed or sad, Caleb."

"If you want me to be happy, go back to the dorm."

I think he actually expects me to stop following him. But I don't. I can't.

For the next ten minutes, I follow him in silence. His pace is slow enough that I can keep up.

"What's the plan?" I ask when we reach the center of town. Every store is closed for the night and the streets are completely dark except for the occasional streetlight. "I hope you have one."

"I don't." He looks defeated.

"We're in this together, at least," I say, in a weak attempt to cheer him up.

"Then let me hold your backpack."

Our footsteps on the sidewalk make a rhythmic sound that echoes through the night. We walk through a residential neighborhood on the edge of town. Every fifteen minutes or so, when Caleb spots a big rock or a bench, he orders me to sit and rest my leg.

"We should stop here," he says when we reach a toddler park. In the middle of the playground is a big wooden castle with jungle gyms, wobbly bridges, and slides attached to every side of the structure. I nod.

Caleb leads me to the castle. We have to crouch down to get through the small entrance. It's hard, but he braces my back and supports me while I maneuver inside the cramped space designed for little kids.

Caleb sits in the corner on wood chips. He pulls a jacket from his duffle and places it on the ground next to him. "Sit next to me," he says. "You can use my leg as a pillow."

I'm glad we stopped. I have no clue what time it is, but the sun isn't up yet and I'm running on fumes.

I see a blue plastic tube sticking out from his duffle. "What's that?" I ask, pointing to it.

He pulls it out and pushes a button. The blue plastic lights up. "It's my lightsaber."

"I remember you used to chase me and Leah around your house with that thing."

"Those were the good ol' days." Caleb waves the lightsaber around, lighting up the inside of the castle.

I reach out and take the lightsaber from him. "You think I'd be a good warrior?" I ask.

"No. You follow the enemy too closely."

"You're not the enemy," I tell him, then bring the lightsaber down to strike his leg.

He catches the lightsaber in his hand before it reaches its intended destination. Our eyes meet, and the bright blue light illuminates both our faces. "I am the enemy, Maggie. You just haven't realized it yet."

"You're wrong." When he turns the lightsaber off and stashes it back in his duffle, I lean into him and get into as comfortable a position as I can. "Wouldn't it be cool if this was a real castle?"

"Only if I was the king of it." He looks up at the sky. "But I'd prefer a castle with a roof over it."

"We can pretend, can't we?"

"Yeah, we can pretend."

Pretending is nice, especially when it takes you away from your problems and worries. "Do you ever think of Mrs. Reynolds?"

"She was hilarious." His mouth quirks up, remembering. "I loved the look on your face when she made you wear that dress to plant flowers in."

"It was a muumuu."

"It was ugly as sin."

"I know. I think of her every day. If it wasn't for her…"

"If it wasn't for her, you probably wouldn't be here lying in wood chips with an ex-con running from the law. You'd be in a warm bed back in the dorm."

"I like it here with you better."

He shakes his head. "You're crazy, you know that?"

"Yep."

He puts his arm around me. "Go to sleep. I know you're tired."

"What about you?"

"My mind is racing and I won't be able to sleep tonight, so you should."

I nestle into his lap and try to forget why and how we got into this situation. I just keep telling myself that it'll be okay. We'll figure a way to work it out. In the end, I'll make sure Caleb reunites with his family in Paradise. I don't know exactly how I'm going to orchestrate it, but I will.

I have to.

"Are you still mad at me?" I murmur against his thigh.

"Definitely."

"What can I do to make you less mad?"

"Stay the hell away from me, Maggie."

"Is that really and truly what you want?" I ask.

"Don't make me answer that question," he says, chuckling cynically.

"Why not?"

"Maggie, I gotta tell you something." I notice that the frown lines on his face are pronounced.

"What?"

"Being with you was never a mistake." He gives a short laugh. "Hell, being with you kept me sane while I was home. You and Mrs. Reynolds made being in Paradise bearable."

I reach up and stroke his stubble with the tips of my fingers. "Thanks, Caleb. I needed to hear that. I know I'm not ideal, and I'll never be normal—"

"Maggie, don't ever say that, okay?"

"But—"

"There are no buts. You're here with me, and I don't fucking deserve your time, let alone your support. I lied to you, I deceived you, and I left you. Why you're here with me is beyond my comprehension."

"You know why I'm here," I tell him. "I believe in you."

"Yeah, well that makes one of us." Without another word, he wraps his arms around me and holds me tight. "I'm sorry I lied to you," he whispers.

"I know you are."

Feeling safe with Caleb's arm around me, I let myself relax and get really sleepy.

He brushes stray hairs out of my face. The last thing I remember is Caleb lightly tracing random patterns on my arm, leg, and back. It feels so good I let myself drift to sleep.

He hasn't changed. He's the same boy I fell in love with back in Paradise.

I love you.

The words hover on the tip of my tongue, and I feel my lips frame the syllables, but no sound comes out as my eyelids droop and Caleb gently strokes my hair over and over again.

In the morning, I wake to find him watching me.

"Morning," I say as I stretch. My leg is retaliating from sleeping on the rough wood chips, but I try and hide the pain from him. "Do we have a plan yet?"

"Yeah, I've got a plan," he says. "But you're not gonna like it."

SEVENTEEN

Caleb

Maggie sits up and bites her bottom lip. She's got wood chips stuck in her hair and her eyes are all bloodshot. "Don't you think we should discuss the plan together?"

"No," I say stoically.

"Why not?"

"Because you're not rational."

"*I beg your pardon,*" she says, wood chips falling from her hair with each word. "But I'm the one who actually slept last night. You've had no sleep. I vote that I'm the rational one, and I vote that we discuss this *together.*"

I stand and hold out my hand to her. "You've never been rational. And before you go begging my pardon again, you were the one who ran off with me in the middle of the night with just a backpack full of stuff."

She takes my hand and lets me help her up. I can tell she's not steady, so I hold her by the waist and support her while her body adjusts.

When she's steady, I let her go. She folds her arms on her chest and puts that straight, aristocratic nose of hers in the air. There isn't a lot of space in this castle, so our bodies brush against each other. "That wasn't irrational. Leaving with you was a calculated risk."

"Calculated?" I ask, skepticism lacing my voice.

"Just forget it." She picks up her backpack and grabs my hand for support as she maneuvers out of the castle. It's early but there are already a few moms with their kids on the playground. They give us dirty looks, as though we were caught fooling around inside the castle's walls.

"So what's this plan you have that I'm not going to like?"

"I'll tell you later," I say.

"You're just stalling the inevitable."

"I know. I'm good at that."

I can tell Maggie's leg is stiff by the way she's walking slowly and tentatively stepping on her left foot. Man, I wish I could take the pain myself. It sucks knowing she'll always have that limp.

Anger at what my sister did to Maggie rushes through me. If it weren't for Leah's irresponsible choice of getting into that car when she'd been drinking, maybe she wouldn't have swerved so much when that squirrel jumped in front of her and Maggie wouldn't have been hit.

I can play the "what if" game forever, but it won't change the fact that Maggie is the one who'll always have the physical repercussions of that night. Nothing I do or say will ever change that.

"Do you need to sit down?" I ask, silently kicking myself because I've put her in this situation.

"I'm okay. Walking usually helps lessen the cramping."

I take her backpack and sling my own duffle over my shoulder. I shake my head as I watch her struggle.

She stops and puts her hand on her hip. "Don't look at me like that."

"Like what?"

"Like you blame yourself. We both know … well, actually, now *everyone* at Re-START knows, that it's not your fault at all even though you've been paying for it for almost two years." Her eyes take on this look of pity, which doesn't sit well in my gut. "Just point me to the nearest place I can go to the bathroom and get some breakfast. I'm starving. I've got about two hundred dollars to spend before we have to beg for money."

Her words slice right through me. "You're not begging for money. *Ever.* Got it? I've got about twenty bucks. After that, I'll figure something out." Just the picture in my head of her having to beg for anything makes my skin crawl.

"I was kidding," she says, surprising me with a grin. "I'm not the begging type."

"Sorry," I say. Sorry for overreacting. Sorry for putting her in this situation. Sorry for every fucking thing.

We walk a couple of blocks until we get to Pete's Place, a little diner which should probably be condemned by the look of the grease-and-mildew-stained ceiling tiles, but they've got a free bathroom and dirt cheap food, and that's what we need. After we get seated in a booth and Maggie heads for the bathroom, I sit back and think about how I'm going to break the news of my plan to her.

I look around at the two other occupied tables. A guy with a ripped flannel shirt is sipping a cup of coffee by the counter. An old guy is eating alone in another booth, looking out the window as he takes one slow bite of his bread after another. I wonder what he's looking at or waiting for ... or if staring out the window is better than remembering that he's alone at a diner eating by himself. Or maybe he's not really looking out the window. Maybe he's daydreaming about some girl he loved and lost.

I don't want to end up like either of those guys—alone and pathetic.

When Maggie comes back, her ponytail is gone. She doesn't look like she slept on a bed of wood chips anymore. She slides into the booth opposite me. I reach across the table and take both her hands in mine. The fact that she was willing to walk away with me last night with just a backpack humbles me.

"Maggie ..." I get a lump in my throat the size of a grapefruit. I don't want to say it, but dammit, it has to be said. "I'm taking you back." Her eyes grow big and she opens her mouth I'm sure to protest, but I add, "Do you know what it does to me every time I see you wince in pain?"

She pulls her hands away and lays them in her lap. "I'm fine."

"Stop pretending. I thought we weren't gonna lie to each other anymore."

I watch as she bites her bottom lip. "Okay, I'm lying. But I don't care if I've got a little discomfort or pain." She looks up at me and tilts her head. I can tell the wheels are turning and she's thinking too much. She hesitates at first, but then blurts out, "Have you ever told a girl you loved her? Not like your mom, but like—"

"You mean Kendra."

"Yeah. I mean Kendra."

That's a loaded question. Kendra told me on our first date that she was in love with me. It didn't take long before we were a couple and were making out ... and not long after that we had sex. Lots of it. She spouted the word "love" as if it was water. I don't think I've heard or said the word "love" since I was arrested.

I did tell Kendra I loved her, but I'm not even sure I knew what it meant at the time.

"Why do you want to know?"

She shrugs. "I just do. You've never said it ..."

She doesn't finish her sentence, but I know what she was going to say. I don't want to go there. Not now ... but after what she's done for me, I can't totally avoid the subject. She deserves that much.

"I don't say it to anyone, which is why you're going back to Re-START. I can't let you come with me. It's not safe and you don't deserve this. You're going to Spain, like you've always wanted. If I said the L-word, it would change everything. I know you, Maggie. You'd feel obligated to stay here and ditch your plans. I'd feel like shit for making you change your life for me... it's not worth it."

I'm not worth it.

The waitress brings the eggs and toast we ordered then disappears just as quickly as she appeared.

Maggie smiles sheepishly from across the table as she picks up her fork. "So come to Spain with me. I'm registered to be an exchange student for my freshman year. It's only for nine months."

"You know I can't. What am I gonna do there, sit and watch you study? I didn't even graduate high school and I hardly know a lick of Spanish."

"You could get a GED and apply."

I shake my head. As if that's even an option at this point. I'm a lost cause with a pathetically bleak future, and hardly a penny to my name. "Oh, sure, then we could get married and live happily ever after if you'll hop on my flying carpet and rub the genie lamp I have in my duffle. Maybe we could buy a Spanish castle while we're at it."

When my dad married my mom, he was going to school to be a dentist and she was president of the ladies' auxiliary. Everything in their lives was strategically planned, up until the day I got arrested and went to jail. "My mom would shit if she heard this conversation."

"I was going to tell you this earlier, but I didn't know how. Caleb, your mom was in rehab when I left Paradise."

My entire body tenses. "I don't want to talk about her. I don't want to talk about my family *at all*."

A bell over the diner door makes me look to see what other misfit is about to patronize Pete's Place. A big black guy comes walking toward us.

Damon.

I'm busted.

I shake my head in frustration and look over at her. "You didn't."

"I did." She holds up her cell phone. "I suspected you were about to run off and ditch me."

I can't *fucking* believe this. "You sold me out. What happened to your desperate plea to make decisions together?"

"You weren't being rational, Caleb," she tries to tell me, her tone too calm, like she's talking to a little kid. Or a crazy person.

"Maybe you heard me wrong. I said *you* weren't rational."

As I watch Damon walk toward us, I contemplate how I'm going to get out of here.

Damon slides in the booth beside me, blocking my escape. "How are my two Re-START runaways doing?" He looks down at my plate of half-eaten food. "Come on,

Mr. Becker, eat up. You'll need your strength for the busy day ahead of us."

I don't touch my plate or look at Damon. I just stare right at Maggie.

"You were going to bring me back to the dorms and leave again." She looks unsure and worried. Good. I want her to suffer. She betrayed me. "I couldn't let you run away again," she says.

"So better to have me locked up, right?"

"That's not what I meant. You can't just run away from people who care about you."

"If you *cared*," I say through clenched teeth, "my damn transition counselor wouldn't be sitting next to me right now."

The waitress comes by to take Damon's order. "I'll have coffee and, uh, just give me another plate of whatever these kids ordered," he tells her.

I stare out the window like the old man in the other booth. Now I know how he feels, wanting to forget the here and now. Why can't Maggie understand my situation? Doesn't she get that I lost what little honor I had by blurting out I wasn't the one who hit her?

Shit.

I need to get away from the truth, away from my past. I need a fresh start.

Except there's no such thing as a fresh start, not when people from your past keep popping up and hounding you, driving home all your mistakes even further. I thought

I'd done a good thing for Leah when I took the fall for her, but what did I really get? No hero's welcome when I came back home, that's for damn sure. The lies are starting to blur with the truth, and Maggie's stuck smack dab in the middle of it.

"All right, kids. Let's have it all out on the table right here and right now. Who was driving the car that hit Maggie?" Damon fishes his cell phone out of his pocket and puts it on the table in front of him. "If you both don't start talking, I'm calling the prosecutor's office. We can handle this my way or their way. Which is it?"

EIGHTEEN

Maggie

Caleb is really mad at me. He turns away and looks out the window. I know he wants to escape right now, which is why I'm so thankful that Damon is here. Physically I can't stop Caleb from leaving, but Damon can.

"Let Damon help you," I say.

Caleb tenses. "Nobody can help, Maggie. Get it through that thick skull of yours, okay?"

"She's not the enemy," Damon says in a terse voice. "Man, kid, you are one master of displaced anger."

"Be careful," Caleb says. "She's a wolf in sheep's clothing. This is your party, Maggie. Why don't you tell Damon everything he wants to know?"

"It's not my story to tell. It's yours."

While Damon eats, Caleb and I are silent.

"I'm waiting," Damon says as he reaches for the salt shaker.

"I can't tell you," Caleb says.

Damon takes a long sip of coffee before very deliberately setting his mug back on the table. "Why not?"

Caleb looks at me, his eyes bleak.

Damon drums his fingers on the tabletop. "I read the file, Caleb. You gave a detailed story about how you swerved to avoid a squirrel, hit Maggie, and panicked."

"I'm a good storyteller," Caleb mumbles.

The drumming stops. "Why did you take the blame for someone else?"

"I don't know."

"That's not an answer."

"Well, that's the only one you're gonna get out of me," Caleb says defiantly.

A squad car drives by the diner, making my heart beat in overtime. Did Damon call the police before he came? Caleb was right, I shouldn't have called Damon.

"Please don't have him arrested," I tell Damon. "Caleb has been punished enough."

"Tell you what," Damon says. "I'll forget I heard about your little secret for now and you finish my Re-START program. If you do, and promise to go back to Paradise and straighten everything out, I'll make sure you stay out of jail for the drug charges. Sound like a deal?"

"Why would you do that?" Caleb asks.

"Let's just say I think you're a good kid. That doesn't mean I think you make stellar choices in life. I think you've made some damn stupid ones, not to mention the little disappearing act you and Maggie pulled last night. But I made some crappy choices as a teen and I'm willing to give you one last chance. You with me?"

"I'm with you," I say, trying to sound cheery.

"What kind of crappy choices?" Caleb asks, challenging Damon. "You sit back and watch all of the Re-START crew tell our fucked-up stories, but you never say a damn word."

Damon picks up his mug and grips it tightly. "I was a coke addict, and I lost everything. I lost my girlfriend, my kid, and my money. One day I didn't pay my supplier for the coke I used and they beat me up real bad. Luckily, I got out, but not a day goes by when I don't regret treating my girl and my kid like they were garbage. I'd do anything to get them back, but it's too late now. She moved to Arizona and lets me see my kid once a year."

"Can't you get them back?" Caleb asks. "Tell them you got your life on track and want to be a family?"

"It's not that simple. I did horrible things—I stole money and property from family and friends. Some things can't be forgiven, and I've come to terms with it. She's moved on. I have to, also. So now that you know my story, are you coming with me?"

Caleb gives me a look that tells me he doesn't trust me anymore, but he's resigned to his fate. "I guess I'm with you, too."

Back at the dorm, we find the rest of the group in the lounge area waiting for us.

"Where did you two sneak off to?" Lenny asks. "A secret rendezvous to do the nasty?"

Caleb and I ignore him. Damon walks up to Lenny and smacks the back of his head while the girls follow me to my room.

"I'm glad you're back," Erin says.

"Me too."

Trish sits on the edge of my bed while I unpack the stuff from my backpack. "Where'd you guys go?"

"Nowhere special. Caleb needed to get away, and I couldn't let him go alone."

When we first walked off campus, I thought that was it for us and Re-START. But even before I knew Caleb was going to make me come back, I realized I couldn't run away. One night in that playground castle proved I couldn't physically do it...I can't leave even if I want to.

"Caleb needs you," Trish says.

I smile weakly. "I don't think he'd agree with you right now. He's pissed that I called Damon to come get us."

"He'll get over it if he knows what's good for him. He probably just needs some time to realize he has to rely on other people. Guys are control freaks and hate when other people know what's best for them."

Damon calls us out in the living room after we're all showered and dressed. He's got a clipboard tucked under one arm and claps his hands together kinda...excited. "We're going to juvie," he announces.

"Been there, done that," Caleb mumbles under his breath.

"It's time to share your stories with troubled teens who are locked up." Damon eyes us over the clipboard in his hands. "Maybe when they get out they'll think twice before getting drunk, or doing drugs, or showing off to their buddies before getting behind the wheel of a car."

Damon walks over to Caleb and gets into his personal space. He doesn't touch him; he just stands there. "You'll be okay, Caleb."

Caleb turns his face away, but as if he can't help the words from coming out against his will he says, "I don't want to go back there, Damon. Cut me some slack, will ya?"

I know how hard it is for Caleb to ask anyone for a favor. I know how much that request cost him.

Damon shakes his head slowly and pats him on the back. "It's important, Caleb. And we'll all be there for you."

In the van, I purposely sit next to Caleb in the back row. The muscles in his jaw are twitching and he's got his hands folded on his chest. He's tense.

"Want to talk about it?" I ask him quietly so nobody else can hear.

"No comment." He looks out the window, shutting me out.

It takes us almost two hours to reach the juvenile detention center, or DOC—Department of Corrections— as Caleb calls it. Our van is cleared and ushered through the tall barbed-wire gate. I can feel the tension and stress radiating off Caleb. He doesn't want to be here. I don't know everything that happened to him here, but a while back he gave me a few glimpses into what he went through.

I'm having second thoughts about calling Damon and telling him we were at the diner. Maybe I should have let things stay as they were. At least then I wouldn't have Caleb mad at me.

"I'm sorry I made you come back to Re-START," I mumble.

"Whatever," he says as he stares out the window at the barbed-wire fence surrounding the compound. "It's over and done."

"What's over and done? Ditching Re-START, or us as a couple?"

A man and woman in dark suits are in the parking lot, waiting for us. We all step out of the van, but Caleb stops me when everyone else is out but us.

"Listen," he says. "I'm not gonna say I haven't thought about what it would be like if you and I, well, you know. But I think we should cool it for a while. At least until after this Re-START bullshit is over."

"And after it's over, what then?"

Damon pounds on the side of the van, startling me. "Come on, slowpokes, get a move on!" Damon yells. "You're holding everyone else up!"

I step out into the hot summer air and stare at the guards with guns in their holsters. It makes me feel safe and scared at the same time.

The guy with the suit walks right up to Caleb. "We haven't seen your mug here since you got released. I trust you're staying out of trouble."

Caleb almost stands at attention, his face as grave as I've ever seen it. He barks out an "I'm trying to, sir," which makes the guy in the suit narrow his eyes at Caleb.

"Try? I'm sure you can do better than try, Becker."

"Yes, sir."

After staring Caleb down, the guy paces in front of all of us. "I'm Mr. Yates and this is Ms. Bushnell," he says loudly, so that we can all hear him. He points to the woman standing next to him, her hair pulled back into a tight bun. "The girls will be visiting our female population with Ms. Bushnell and the boys will be visiting our male population with me. You ready?"

We all nod, except Caleb. I watch as he pulls Damon aside and says quietly, "I can't do this."

NINETEEN

Caleb

"I can't do this," I tell Damon again. Shit, my knee has been shaking nonstop since he started driving.

Damon pats me on the back again, as if he's a friend of mine and will stand by me no matter what. "Yes, you can. Trust me."

Trust him? When was the last time I actually trusted anyone without getting screwed? "Whatever, dude."

"Listen, you're stronger than you think, Caleb. These kids are looking for role models."

I swipe sweat off my forehead. "Get a clue, Damon. I'm not a role model, and I don't want to be one. What am I gonna tell these guys, that I went to jail for something I didn't do?"

"It's your choice what you tell them."

I look up at the brick building that I lived in for almost a year. I had to get up at six thirty and shower in front of others, I had to eat when they said eat, and when I needed to use the facilities during juvie school, I was escorted into the bathroom so I could crap. It was pathetic.

Just like back then, it doesn't seem like I have any choice in the matter. I follow Yates and the other Re-START guys towards the male sector, but look back and watch Ms. Bushnell escort the girls to the other sector. Maggie is limping behind her. Very soon she's going to see the reality of how I lived for a year. I wish I could stop her from going in there.

When I was in the DOC, the girls and guys never saw each other. We had school a few hours a day, went to group therapy, were assigned chores, went outside for an hour, ate three meals, and had the rest of the day to chill in our cells. We were encouraged to read a lot or study to pass the time, but a lot of the guys hated reading or couldn't read worth shit.

In the intake center waiting room, my hands are shaking a little, so I shove them into my pockets as I stand and scan the security guards and security cameras and securely locked doors. I glance at the waiting cells, where you get locked up before they register you. Bad memories come flooding back.

After registering as an offender here, they confiscate every single piece of clothing and personal item and keep them locked up until you're released. The strip search is next, and let me tell you, the guard who does it makes sure you're not hiding any contraband in any crevice of your body.

Yates holds out a clear plastic bin. "Empty all your pockets. I mean *everything*, including pens, pencils, money, wallets, and paper."

We all do as instructed, then we're escorted through a bunch of locked doors and corridors. We come to a room where inmates meet their families and friends on visitors' day.

"We've decided to pair you off," Yates says. "You'll each be meeting with our residents one-on-one. That way, we can have shifts and you guys can share your stories in a small setting. No cussing or lewd comments are allowed. No touching the residents."

Damon, Matt, and I all look over at Lenny, who puts his hand on his chest. "You guys think I'm lewd?"

Is he kidding me? The kid urged me to pull his finger so he could fart, he fans his sweaty ball sacks in front of us, and doesn't clean his wayward pubes off the toilet seat. If *he's* not lewd, God help us all.

I roll my eyes.

"No comment," Matt says and laughs.

Damon gives Lenny a sharp stare. "Keep it appropriate, Lenny, or you'll find yourself on bathroom cleaning duty for the rest of the day."

Lenny mocks Damon by saluting him. "Yes, sir."

Damon shakes his head. He's probably counting down the days until this program is over and he can kick us to the curb.

Yates sits on the edge of one of the tables in the room and points to me. "Caleb will attest to the fact that some of our residents come from broken homes and/or gangs and don't have a grounded filter when it comes to making good choices. A lot of these kids will trust you if you've also gone through tough times like they have. They think hardships are a badge of honor."

My hardships are a pain in my ass, not a badge of honor. And make no mistake about it, the guys locked in the DOC are far from *residents*. Yates makes it sound like these guys are paying rent for their living quarters. What a fucking joke. In reality, they're locked up like animals.

We're each assigned a table. It's eerily quiet as the first round of inmates join us. They walk in the room with their hands behind their backs as required by the guards, their expressions blank. The familiar dark blue polyester jumpsuits take me back to the first day I was here. That suit was a constant reminder my life was not my own anymore ... while I was locked up, it was owned by the Illinois Juvenile Justice Department and the Department of Corrections.

Their heads are all buzz-cut or shaved, a requirement for all new inmates. When the final person walks in the room, it's like a ghost appears right in front of me.

It's Julio, my old cellmate. He's wearing an orange jumpsuit instead of the regular blue one, meaning he's under harsh restrictions for getting into trouble in the DOC.

I haven't heard from or talked to Julio since I left this place. He was a complete ass when we were first assigned as cellmates, but after he realized I wasn't afraid of him and saw me stand toe-to-toe with gang member Dino Alvarez in the exercise yard when he cornered me, we got along just fine.

Julio, tattoos on his neck peeking out of his suit, sits opposite me. "Long time no see, *amigo*."

"How you been?" I ask.

"Chillin' in the DOC. I get released in two weeks, if not sooner," he says with a grin. "Hoo-rah. Just got to stay out of trouble."

Not easy for a guy like Julio.

Julio was the one who hooked me up with his cousin Rio. I lived with Rio until... "Rio got busted."

Julio shakes his head. "I heard. Fuckin' shame. My cuz ain't gettin' out anytime soon 'cause he's a repeater. I'm screwed too, 'cause I was gonna live with him. My ma moved back to Mexico with her boyfriend."

"I got busted too," I tell him. "That's why I'm on this program. It was either this, or get locked up again."

I watch Julio lean back in his chair as the news sinks in. "What you gonna do after you're done?"

I shrug. "Don't know."

Damon walks over to us. "Sounds like a reunion, guys."

"Julio was my cellmate," I explain. "Julio, this is Damon. He was my transition counselor."

Julio nods to Damon and shuts up immediately. There's no way Julio is gonna be friendly or chat with anyone who works for the DOC in any way, shape, or form. Julio is a gang member with connections inside and outside this place, and he doesn't trust anyone outside of his circle. I'm surprised he still trusts me, but then again we spent almost a year as cellmates and slept, ate, and shit in close quarters.

Damon walks over to Matt's table. Matt is talking to a kid who looks like the typical newbie. He's scared as hell to be here but is putting on a tough front.

A guard stands right by the solid metal door, a stun gun on one side of his belt and a shoot-to-kill gun on the other. I notice that one of the guards has his eyes trained on Julio. This isn't the typical juvie. This place holds big-time offenders who just happen to be underage. Yates is on the opposite side of the room, his arms folded on his chest as he narrows his eyes at us. They're watching us like hawks like they did when I was an inmate here.

Julio leans in and whispers, "Yates thinks this shithole is the Club Med, but it sucks. I can't wait to get out of here, man. Hell, maybe I'll come visit you in Paradise. I've always wanted to know how the hicks in the boondocks live. I hear the chicks in Paradise are easy."

"Some are," I say, thinking about my ex, Kendra, "and some aren't," I add, thinking about Maggie.

My thoughts turn to Maggie. She's probably freaking out meeting tough girls who eat innocent girls like her for breakfast.

Yates passes our table and gives us the evil eye.

What does the guy expect, that I'll slip Julio some drugs or a shovel so he can dig his way out of here?

I clear my throat and lean toward Julio. "So I'm supposed to share how reckless driving has changed my life and caused pain to others. It's part of the program."

Julio rolls his eyes and snorts. "All right, hit me with it."

"Reckless driving changed my life and caused pain to others," I say, as if I'm reading off a cue card.

Julio grins. I'm making a joke of this visit and Julio gets it. But the truth is, it's not a joke. It's reality. Suddenly, I get serious.

I take a deep breath and let it out slowly. "I guess I, um, never told you what really happened the night I was arrested."

"You never talked much about it."

"Yeah, 'cause I didn't do it." I shrug and look at my former cellmate. "I pled guilty even though I wasn't guilty."

Julio chuckles. "You're shittin' me, right?" He says it low so nobody can hear him cuss. Yates doesn't take cussing lightly, not in his jail. Luckily Warden Miller isn't here, or Julio would probably get some sort of punishment for cussing. Warden Miller takes his rules seriously and expects everyone else to. If not, you better be prepared for extra chores, early bedtime, or even solitary.

I shake my head. "Nope."

"Why'd you plead guilty? To protect someone?"

"Yeah," I whisper. "Something like that."

"Wow. Can't say I'd do the same thing." Julio looks at me sideways. "Unless it was family. I'd die for my family."

I nod slowly. "Me too."

Julio nods back in complete understanding, because even though we come from totally different backgrounds, we're cut from the same cloth. He knows just by my nod that I sacrificed myself and went to jail for a family member.

"You regret it?" he asks.

I pause to think about what my life would have been like if I hadn't been arrested. "Yeah, I do. Fucked-up thing is, I can't say I wouldn't do it again."

"Loyalty and honor and all that shit really screws with your head, doesn't it?"

"Yeah." I wince, because images of Maggie aren't far from my thoughts. I don't want to think about her now. "And girls really screw with your head, too."

Julio raises an excited eyebrow. "My boy Caleb's got a girl? Nice goin', dude. Who is she? Last I heard, you and your skanky ex broke up 'cause she was gettin' it on with your best friend."

"One more minute guys," Yates bellows. "Wrap it up!"

"I don't have a girl," I say, chuckling at the thought. "Besides, the only chick I might want hates me. I never say the right thing around her. Hell, I try and push her away so I don't have to deal with the drama. And she pisses me off most of the time."

"Sounds like a match made in Heaven to me." Julio

leans across the table. "Take advice from a guy who hasn't seen a girl under twenty in over a year—the only female I've talked to lately is the cafeteria worker, and she's so fugly I'm not even sure she's female. You only live once, so take advantage of what you got when you have it."

"You too."

"I hear you loud and clear. No regrets anymore, okay? Live every day like it's your last. *¿Comprende?*"

Yates orders the inmates to line up at the door.

I crack a smile. Julio is right. I've been living every day with regret, when it should be the other way around. "Yeah, I understand."

"See you on the outside, Caleb." He holds up two fingers. "Peace." With those words, he shuffles out of the room.

I'm ready to live my life without regrets. I've just got to figure out a strategy to make that happen.

TWENTY

Maggie

I'm sitting across from a girl with dyed-blonde hair and dark roots. She's wearing blue sweatpants and a blue T-shirt like the other girls in jail. Ms. Bushnell assigned her to my table. The girl is staring at me as if she doesn't want to be here.

"I'm Maggie," I tell her.

"So, Maggie, what's your story?" she asks impatiently, totally uninterested.

I tell her how I was hit by a car in a hit-and-run accident and spent a year in hospitals and rehab. Her eyes glaze over and at one point I think she might be falling asleep.

When I explain how I didn't fit in when I came back to start my senior year of high school, she asks, "Is that supposed to make me feel sorry for you? Listen, I've got more to deal with than a busted-up leg. My dad's a drunk, and my mom walked out on us five years ago. I'm not really crying over your limp, so you might as well save your breath and the rest of your story for someone who actually gives a shit."

I didn't get much sleep last night. Caleb's not talking to me. I'm crabby and my nerves are on edge. If this girl doesn't want to have sympathy, fine. But that doesn't mean I have to sit here while she patronizes me.

"*You* listen," I say, then lean across the table so I've got her undivided attention and to make sure she hears me loud and clear. "Just because you've got a bad home life doesn't give you the right to sit there and be rude."

"Sure it does," she fires back. "I bet you've got parents with money—"

"My mom works as a waitress in a diner."

"Well I bet your dad ain't a drunk—"

"I wouldn't know," I tell her. "My dad walked out on my mom. I haven't seen him in years. Oh, and I forgot to mention that I fell for the guy who went to jail for hitting me with his car. I wasn't supposed to be talking to him in the first place. Then he came on this trip, but now he's not talking to me again, and I'm supposed to pretend like we're just friends and I'm afraid of losing him although I know that's stupid because I feel like I've already lost him ... and none of it would have happened if it weren't for a reckless driving incident. So when you get out of this place, please don't drive recklessly or you might end up with a permanent disability, boyfriendless, and an outcast at school."

Instead of the girl falling asleep or giving me attitude, she's now staring at me wide-eyed. "All right. You made your point. I get it."

"Thanks," I tell her, and mean it.

"Does it suck when people stare at you when you walk?" she asks.

At first when I got out of the hospital I didn't even want to get out of my wheelchair and walk, because I knew I drew more stares from my ridiculously pronounced limp than being confined to a wheelchair. I hated the stares.

"I hate being stared at, but I try and block it out," I tell her. "I admit it makes me feel like I'm the main event at a freak show." I look down and say what I don't like to put into words but it's the honest truth. "There's not a day goes by that I wish the accident hadn't happened and that I could be normal. It's on my mind every day."

"Not a day goes by where I don't regret doin' what I done to get myself locked up in here," she says.

"I don't know if I can ask you questions about why you're here."

"Let's just say I hurt someone *real bad*," she tells me, then focuses at a spot on the wall. Maybe she doesn't want to see my reaction.

I look at the female guard blocking the door and Ms. Bushnell on the opposite end of the room. They're eyeing the inmates. I wonder if there's ever a time they're not being watched or evaluated. I think of Caleb, who told me he hated being watched by guards every second of the day. I wonder how he's holding up now, being here again.

"It must be horrible being in here," I mumble.

The girl shrugs. "Actually it ain't that bad. Beats bein' home. I guess I hate bein' here 'cause it reminds me of what I done. I hurt this girl. The memories of that night give me nightmares most nights. I was thinkin' about writin' her a letter, but she'd prob'ly throw it out and never read it."

"You could try. If anything it'll probably make you feel better to write it down."

"I don't think so."

"Just think about it."

"You have one more minute, ladies!" Ms. Bushnell announces loudly. "Say your good-byes and line up at the door."

"Yeah, well, I guess it was cool meeting you," the girl says. "The girls who don't got no visitors got to come to talk to you guys. It sucks when it's visiting day and nobody calls out your name that you got a visitor, so, uh, thanks for bein' here." She clears her throat. "I'm Vanessa. My friends back home called me V, but to be honest I don't got no friends anymore."

I raise my hand. Ms. Bushnell walks over to our table. "Is there a problem?" she asks.

"No," I'm quick to tell her. "I just wanted to know if I could have Vanessa's address … so we can be pen pals."

Ms. Bushnell's stern face softens. "That would be fine. I'll give you the information before you leave the building."

"You didn't have to go an' do that," Vanessa says when Ms. Bushnell walks away.

"I know."

Vanessa smiles, the first smile I've seen from her since she walked in the room. "You're okay, Maggie. And if you do ever write me, I promise to write back. Just don't expect no fancy writin'."

"It's a deal."

"And just so you know, I don't think you're a freak at all. In fact, I think you're one of the coolest girls I've ever met."

I smile. "I'm a geek," I tell her.

"No you're not." She points her finger at me. "You, Maggie, are one cool chick. Don't forget it."

A cool chick? "Nobody has ever called me cool before."

"That's 'cause you don't act it. If you think you're cool and act like you're the shit, everyone'll start treating you like you've got it goin' on. You get what I'm sayin'?"

"I think so."

"Don't waste a single day thinkin' you're a geek, or you might as well be locked in here like me."

Vanessa and the other girls get in a single file line by the locked metal door with their hands held behind their backs. Some of the girls look really young … like they're barely in high school or even younger than that. The guard leads them out. Before Vanessa leaves, she looks back and gives me a small good-bye nod.

According to Vanessa, my limp and scars don't matter. I'm a cool chick. I just have to start believing it.

Our whole Re-START group is quiet as we leave the DOC. I head for the back of the van where Caleb usually sits, but when he sees me, he slides into the front row next to Trish.

I'm stuck in the back with Lenny.

When we get back to Dixon Hall, Damon tells us we have two days off to rest and have fun. Matt suggests we go to Independence Grove tomorrow to rent canoes and fish in the lake.

Caleb seems really distant since we left the detention center. I wonder what happened with him on the guys' side of the jail. I don't find out, though, because Caleb spends the rest of the evening alone in his room. Damon calls him to the lounge area for dinner.

"I'll just grab something from the fridge later," he says. When we're about to watch a movie in the lounge, I peek in and see him lying on his bed, staring at the ceiling.

"Caleb, we're watching a movie."

"Watch without me."

"Are you okay?" I ask tentatively. "Want to talk?"

He gives a short laugh and shakes his head.

"Are you going to be mad at me forever?"

He doesn't answer.

The next morning, as we're all rubbing on sunscreen, Caleb is the last to get ready. He slaps on a baseball cap, long shorts, and a tank top. Caleb's tattoo reminds me of black flames licking his skin. It makes him look tough and untouchable, which I'm sure was the look he was going for when he got it.

At the park, Damon buys us worms. He rents fishing gear and three boats, and tells us we're on our own and he'll be back before noon with lunch.

"Hey Trish," Lenny says as he watches her lay out a towel on the sandy beachfront. "Do you know you can see your nipple outline through your bikini top?"

"You're a pig," Trish says, then pushes Lenny away.

Lenny holds his hands up. "What? I was gonna say you have nice nips. Geez, Trish. Get a grip and learn how to take a compliment."

We're all looking at Lenny as if he's out of his mind.

Trish crosses her arms over her chest and makes a big deal of checking out Lenny's lower regions. "Do you know you *can't* see your dick outline through your bathing suit?" She tosses her hair and says, "Just so you know, Lenny, that *wasn't* a compliment."

Without warning, Lenny picks up Trish and carries her into the lake, kicking and screaming.

"You better not throw me in!" she screams, still kicking, as she grabs onto Lenny's neck for dear life.

"Oh, yeah, baby, you're bein' tossed." Lenny says, seemingly oblivious to the kicks and pleas of the girl he's been at odds with since this trip started.

I look over at Caleb, who's watching Lenny and Trish. He turns to me and an evil look crosses his face. He nods, as if Lenny is carrying out the most brilliant punishment to a girl who pissed him off.

"You're not thinking of tossing *me* in the lake," I tell him.

"Yeah," he says. "I am."

TWENTY—ONE

Caleb

This is the first time since I met Lenny that I get a glimpse his brain is capable of making a smart decision.

My mind does the mental gymnastics to justify what I'm thinking: Maggie's leg hinders her on land, but in the water she's just like the rest of us. She really screwed everything up for me by calling Damon. I need to take control of the situation and have no regrets. Which means...

Maggie needs to get wet. And, to use a Damonism: right now.

"Come here," I tell her. I strip off my tank in one swift movement.

She steps back, her bare feet sinking into the sand.

"Promise me you won't toss me in the lake." She glances quickly at the water, then looks back at me. "There's *fish* swimming around in there."

"They won't hurt you."

"I can't swim," she says quickly as she takes another step away from me.

"Caleb, not a good idea," Matt chimes in from beside her.

I give Matt a *you're an idiot* look. "I've known Maggie all my life. Don't let her fool you—she's an excellent swimmer." So much for her being honest with me.

A big splash brings our attention back to Lenny and a now very wet Trish. I take this break in Maggie's concentration to catch her. I lift her and carry her to the water's edge.

"I'm wearing pants!" she screams, wiggling violently. "Let me down! Seriously, Caleb. I'm the shit, so back off!"

I suppress a laugh, 'cause I never expected those words to come out of Maggie. "You're the shit, huh? And all along I thought I was the shit."

I walk further into the water. Her hands are wrapped tight around my neck, locking behind me like a vice.

"Okay, joke's over Caleb. Let me down."

Her head nestles into the crook of my neck, and her wild hair is flying in my face. If I wasn't so angry with her I might be tempted to like the way she's clinging to me.

"Don't throw me in. Promise me."

I go deeper. The sand on the bottom of the lake is

soft, making my feet sink in. The water is up to my knees now. I pass Lenny and Trish, who are splashing each other. They're both soaked.

Maggie and I are about to get soaked too.

"I'm not gonna toss you in," I tell Maggie as I turn into a little bend in the lake for some privacy. Nobody on shore can see us now. "I promise."

She loosens her hold on my neck and leans her head back to look into my eyes. "You're not?" she asks, letting out a sigh of relief.

"No." I hold in my amusement as the next words fly out of my mouth. "But hold your breath or you'll get a mouthful of lake water."

Before she can ask why, I dunk us both. She tries pushing away from me as soon as we come up completely drenched a second later, but I hold onto her tight. I may be pissed at her, but I don't want her drowning from shock, or weighted down because she's wearing long pants.

Maggie comes up sputtering, but not from lake water getting in her mouth. The girl is mad as hell. "How... could...you!"

"It was pretty easy, actually," I tell her, still holding her tight while she tries to push me away.

She splashes my face.

"Don't do that," I tell her.

She does it again, so I let her go. She maneuvers to stand a few feet in front of me, her hands already underneath the water. She's definitely ready for a splash war. I play dirty, though, and splashing is a kids' game. We're not kids anymore.

Maggie is about to get a dose of what it's like to play in the big leagues.

I wade closer to her. She starts splashing, but I don't reciprocate. I'm soaking wet, but I ignore the water hitting in my face and stinging my eyes. I just keep moving closer until I'm close enough to reach out and grab her wrists so she can't splash me anymore.

I hold her hands behind her back and pull her snugly against my body. She's so close I feel her breasts pressed against my bare chest. When she looks up at me, our lips are inches apart. Her hair is dripping wet, her face has droplets of water glistening from the sun reflecting on them, and her lips are shiny and wet.

I don't know how I ever could have thought of this girl as plain.

"What are you gonna do now that I'm helpless?" she asks.

I lean down and whisper in her ear, "You've got it all wrong, Maggie. I'm the helpless one here."

"Oh," she says, eyes wide.

I loosen my hold on her wrists while I slide my lips across her cheek. The sensation of her soft skin against my lips combined with her body still pressed against mine is driving me insane. Oh, hell. I don't want to want her. It would be so much easier to hate Maggie and ban her from my thoughts and my life. But Julio's words echo in my head: no regrets.

When my lips reach the corner of her mouth, I let go of her arms and move my hands to her waist. At the same time, I lightly glide my lips across hers. She sighs and breathes faster as our wet lips slide ever so slowly back and forth, back and forth.

It's erotic. Painfully erotic.

I'm not gonna deepen the kiss, that's her move. I'm gonna make her want it so damn bad she'd rather die than not feel my tongue sliding against hers. She's gotta want this even more than me.

There's one problem here. My body is betraying me, big time. I'm glad we're under water so the evidence of my arousal is hidden from view.

When her hands reach up and sneak around my neck, I know I've got the upper hand. She wants this. I'm gonna make her beg for it and make out with her like there's no tomorrow. Then I'll walk away as if I don't give a shit.

Cruel, yes. But I've got to prove to her once and for all that I'm a badass ex-con. Yesterday at the DOC, seeing Julio and the other inmates reminded me where I came from. Who I really am. Doesn't matter if I didn't hit Maggie and went to jail for my sister.

I'll always be an ex-con. It's branded on me like an invisible tattoo. But I need to live each day like it's my last ... with no regrets.

I hold back a groan as Maggie opens her lips and tilts her head. Her lips slant, slightly open, against mine. This is it. Finally. I'm waiting impatiently for her tongue to snake out and reach mine. It's gonna happen any second. It's *gotta* happen, 'cause this is fucking torture. I know she's no stranger to French kissing. Hell, we did it back at the dorm and it was earth-shattering.

I'm ready. *Damn, I'm more than ready.* My entire body is screaming of readiness. She's got to be ready for this, too.

She opens her mouth wider and moans, a moan that makes me fantasize about what it would be like to witness her having an orgasm. I'm so turned on I know I'm gonna pay for it later.

But that doesn't matter.

I swallow a triumphant smile. Here it comes. That moan of hers was a clue that she's dying to take this to the next level. I wish my body wasn't ready to take this to the next *three* levels.

She moans against my lips again, and my tongue is twitching in my mouth ready to be unleashed like a fucking caged animal. I'm usually a patient kisser, but...

Still nothing.

What the—

I lean back. "What the hell are you doing?"

"What do you mean?" she asks, innocently batting her eyelashes against the hot sun beaming down on us.

Is she *kidding* me?

"Where's your tongue?" I ask stupidly.

Her wet little eyebrows furrow. "In my mouth. Why, where's it supposed to be?"

I let go of her, step back and rub my hands through

my soaked hair to get a handle on reality. "You're fucking with me, right?"

She shrugs. The movement creates ripples around her body that move across the water. "Maybe."

Oh. No. She. Didn't.

My tongue is unleashed now, but it's to argue not to kiss. "You were trying to get me all hot and bothered to get back at me for dumping you in the water, weren't you? *Admit it*. You're not the innocent little Maggie you want everyone to think you are. You're a damn tease, that's what you are."

"And what were you doing, Caleb? Weren't you trying to get me all hot and bothered on purpose? *You're* the tease."

"You have no clue," I bark back. This lying bit can go both ways, sweetheart.

Maggie starts wading toward shore.

I'm left here, all alone. Not how I thought this scenario would go down. "So you're just gonna walk away?"

"Yes," she calls out, her back to me. "You were the one who said we needed to break things off until this trip was over. I'm just following your rules."

I wish I could follow her, but I need to stay waist-deep for at least another minute until my body cools down.

"I said we needed to cool it."

"I'm cool," she says over her shoulder.

"I'm not." I'm all hot and bothered. Being in the cool lake should help, but doesn't.

Maggie one-upped me. My ego is busted, big time. But I manage to forget it for the time being and get out of the water. I lie on the beach and wonder if I need to try a different tactic.

A half hour later, we all head into our little canoes with our fishing gear. None of the girls know how to put a worm on a hook, so each guy has to go with one of the girls.

"I'm going with Matt," Maggie declares up front. Matt is all too eager to accommodate her.

In the end, I'm stuck with Trish, because she says she's afraid Lenny will tip the boat on purpose.

Lenny and poor Erin are paired up, and she looks like she's about to puke. She looks that way most of the time lately. I'm starting to think she's either got a case of the flu or a case of pregnancy.

"So what's the real story with you and Maggie?" Trish asks as we row out to the middle of the lake. "It looks like you two are a couple again."

"We're not."

Trish rolls her eyes. "Oh, puh-lease. It's obvious you guys having something hot and heavy going on. Just spill the beans already so the rest of us don't have to speculate about it anymore."

I laugh. "What've you speculated?"

"That you're still in love with her." She hands me the worm container and her fishing pole. "You want to know what I think?"

"Not really. Why don't we talk about you and Lenny?"

"What about me and Lenny?" she asks, her face scrunched up like I'm nuts.

"Admit you've got a thing for him."

"Eww. Don't make me throw up, Caleb." I put the worm on the hook and Trish winces. "How can you do that? It's inhumane."

"Think of it as feeding the fish."

Trish folds her arms across her chest. "Yeah, right. Feeding them, then sticking a hole in their face as punishment for wanting a little food."

I hand the pole back to her, all ready to go. "You want to fish, or not?" I ask her as I notice Matt and Maggie across the way with their poles in the water. They're talking. I wonder if she's complaining about me.

"She's scared, you know," Trish says. "She thinks you'll leave her again."

"She's probably right."

"Then let her go, Caleb. Stop confusing her and giving her mixed signals. She deserves a guy who'll stick around and be there when she needs him."

"Like Matt?" I say harshly.

Trish holds her hands up. "Don't get all pissed off. I'm just saying what I think."

"I think you should keep your opinions to yourself."

Trish puts her fishing pole into the water and says with certainty, "And I think you know I'm right."

TWENTY—TWO

Maggie

For the rest of the Re-START trip, Caleb keeps his distance. He acts like we're mere acquaintances. He only interacts with me when he has to. When we talk to groups around Illinois, Indiana, and Wisconsin, Caleb shares how he was arrested and how he'd do anything to avoid jail in the future.

He doesn't talk about going to jail for Leah. I think he wants to forget that part of the story, although in my opinion the reality of what he did for his sister looms over him every day. I wish I could get him to talk about it, but at this point he doesn't trust me at all.

I'm not sure he trusts anyone.

It's the day before the end of the trip, and we're staying in a big rented cabin in Lake Geneva, Wisconsin. The cabin has nine bedrooms, so we each get our own. But I can't sleep with the thought of losing Caleb again pressing on me. I peek into his room at two in the morning, but his bed is empty. My heart is panicking, thinking he's skipped out early.

Relief washes over me as I spot Caleb from my window. He's skipping rocks by the lake.

My brain tells me it will be better to just let him go.

My heart ... not so much.

I still want to convince him to go back to Paradise. I haven't done a great job of doing what I set out to do. Tonight is my last chance. Thinking about what Vanessa said, I brace myself to confront Caleb once and for all.

I slip through the sliding glass door. The melodic sound of the crickets chirping follows in my wake as I walk down the gravel path to the lake.

"I guess this is good-bye ... again."

He doesn't look at me. Instead, he skips another rock. "I guess so. Have fun in Spain."

I haven't thought about my impending year abroad for a few weeks now. This Re-START trip has been exhausting both physically and mentally. I've learned a lot about myself this past month. I've also become good friends with Trish and Erin, who are now like sisters. Trish thinks she's Erin's protector, and the three of us have spent most nights talking until the early morning hours.

I sit on a big boulder and watch him. "Where are you headed?"

He shrugs. "Arizona, I think."

Arizona? That's too far. There are so many loose ends he needs to tie up before he goes away. "Come back to Paradise, Caleb."

"This conversation is over."

I stand and step right in front of him. He's about to skip another rock, but I take his hand and open it up so the rock falls to the ground. "Go back to Paradise," I say again.

He lowers his gaze to the ground, and I feel his defeat as if it's my own. "I can't. When I came back home, my entire family wanted me to pretend the Beckers were this picture-perfect family. In reality, each one of us was fucked up. I couldn't fake it before. I still can't, so don't even ask me to. I'm living with so many regrets, I can't add another one to the roster."

"Give them the benefit of the doubt. They need you."

He shakes his head. "I have nothing to go back to. Hell, even Mrs. Reynolds is dead. The only person I'd go back for is you, and we were doomed from the start." He steps away from me and runs his fingers through his hair. He does that when he's frustrated. "Forget I just said I'd go back for you. That was stupid of me."

I'm waiting for him to say our cooling-off period will be over, that he's ready to try again. But he doesn't. Maybe he realized that what we have isn't worth the hassle, especially because I'm leaving for Spain and he's leaving for Arizona.

I think of the times we kissed and held each other. I thought nothing could feel as amazing as I felt then, so powerful and explosive.

"Are you really leaving?" I ask, my voice coming out as a whisper.

"Yeah. No regrets."

"What?" No regrets? "Why do you keep saying that? What does it mean?"

He cups my chin tenderly and urges me to look up at him. "It means I can't leave until I do this…"

He bends his head. I wait for his warm, full lips to meet mine as my heart pounds like crazy in my chest. His lips hover over mine, and we both smile because it brings us back to the lake where we were testing and teasing each other. It was playful and dangerous. We're playing a playful and dangerous game right now, but I tell myself to enjoy it and ignore the warnings in the back of my head.

At least that's what I keep trying to tell myself as I close my eyes and he presses his lips to mine. I savor every moment of our kiss. It's not hot and heavy and hungry. It's slow and sexy and sensual. He takes hold of my waist and pulls me closer.

Oh, God, I want to melt in his arms right here and now. I wrap my arms around his neck as we keep kissing and holding and touching. He lifts me off the ground. I can't imagine anyone else being able to make me feel invincible and beautiful and worthy like Caleb does. I want to scream *I love you, Caleb! Don't you feel what I feel when I'm with you?*

His lips slowly pull away from mine and he unwraps my arms from around his neck. "I won't regret that … ever. Good-bye, Maggie."

"Bye, Caleb. I'll … miss you."

"I'll miss you, too."

I take a deep breath, holding back the flood of emotions. I push past him and hurry toward the cabin so he doesn't see the tears streaming down my cheeks. I quickly get into bed and bury my head into my pillow so he can't hear my heartache as I cry.

Why do I do this? Why do I let him go without a fight? Because I'm a coward, that's why.

I hear the sliding door creak open a few minutes later. Caleb must be back in the cabin. I think of Vanessa, who is stuck in jail and can't fight for what she wants.

I can.

I realize what Caleb's motives were for kissing me tonight. That sweet kiss was an attempt at closure.

It wasn't enough, at least for me. I want more. I need more. But do I have the nerve to show him what kind of closure I want in order to finally let go?

I take a deep breath as I sit on the edge of my bed. I can do this. I'm careful to take soft steps and pray the wooden floor of the cabin doesn't creak as I make my way down to the basement.

To Caleb's room.

His door is open. Lenny is sleeping soundly in the room across the hall. Lenny's snores echo through the walls, but Caleb's room is quiet. I don't even hear him breathing as I step in.

There are no windows, so it's almost completely dark. A green glow is coming from a permanent night-light in the hallway.

"Caleb?" I whisper. "You awake?"

"Yeah." I hear his sheets rustle as he sits up. "Is something wrong?"

"Kind of."

I close the door, then feel my way slowly around the room, hoping I don't trip and fall. I bump into something warm and hard and distinctly male. Caleb. He's not wearing a shirt, because I feel his hot skin and muscular chest against my fingertips.

I look up into the darkness. "Hi."

"Hey," he says, his familiar voice comforting to me somehow. I'm going to miss that voice. "I don't suppose you got lost."

"No. I, uh, couldn't sleep. And I thought... I just... well..."

"What is it, Maggie? Just say it."

Okay. I might as well gather up the nerve. It's now or never. "I thought we could spend our last night together. I know we might not see each other again after tomorrow, but I can't help but want to be in your arms tonight. Just one last time. Is that okay?"

Caleb takes my hand in his and leads me back to his bed. "It's more than okay."

I slip under the covers and wait for him to join me, but he doesn't.

"Where are you going?" I ask.

"To lock the door. You don't want Lenny to suddenly barge in on us, do you?"

I laugh nervously. "No."

It's cool in the basement, so I pull the blanket up to my chest. Caleb slides in beside me, and I feel his bare legs against mine. "You're shivering," he says, his voice a low whisper.

"I'm a little cold … and a little nervous."

"Don't be nervous, Maggie. It's just me."

It's the real Caleb, without the tough facade. I'm glad it's completely dark now and he can't see my trembling fingers as they move up to his beautiful face. "I know."

He pulls me closer. I rest my head in the crook of his arm and am more content than ever.

"Maggie?"

"Yeah?"

"Thanks."

"For what?"

"For making me feel alive again."

I drape my arm across his chest, the warmth of his skin melting into mine. I want to remember this night forever, because we'll probably never get another chance to hold each other like this again. It makes me want to do more than just sleep in his arms. I try and relax, to slow my own erratic heartbeat as I wrap my right leg, the one that wasn't severely damaged in the accident, around him. It's a definite hint that I'm ready to do more than just lie in his arms.

He moans in response. "Maggie, you're treading into dangerous territory. I'm trying to be a good, honorable guy here."

"I know. But I'm not asking you to be one."

"You sure you know what you're getting into?"

"Nope. I've got no clue." I start kissing and feeling my way across his broad chest.

"You're killing me," he says, his hands slowly reaching for me and urging me up so we're face to face. "We can't do this. Don't get me wrong, I'm ready and willing. But we're going in completely different directions tomorrow. You and I both know fooling around or having sex will complicate everything."

"I have a great idea," I say matter-of-factly. "Let's just make out all night until we're exhausted. That's okay, isn't it?"

"Make out, huh?" He pulls me on top of him. "We can definitely do that," he murmurs against my lips.

Afterward, when we're both coming down from a high I've never felt before, I lay my head on his chest while he wraps his arms around me. "That was a great make-out session."

"Mmm," he agrees sleepily. "The best." A few minutes later, I feel Caleb's body relax. His slow, even breathing lulls me to sleep.

TWENTY-THREE
Caleb

I slept like the dead last night. Maggie's soft, warm body snuggled up to me was just the sleeping pill I needed after our little (okay, not so little) make-out fest. I knew the second she snuck out of my room this morning, because I was immediately awake when the cool morning air reached my skin.

I pretended not to wake up, even when she lightly kissed me on the lips.

Breakfast was practically torture, because Maggie and I were both trying to avoid eye contact. Damon called us into the main area of the cabin, where he gave an entire half hour speech about how much he respected all of us for finishing the program, even though he knew how hard it was to share our stories.

During the ride back to the Redwood community center, where this whole trip started, we're all pretty silent. Even Lenny. His solemn attitude is unnerving because it's so out of character. At this point I'm tempted to ask if I could pull his finger.

At the community center, Damon pulls me aside.

"You're going back home, right?" he asks. "You promised."

"Yep," I lie. "I'm gonna come clean to my parents. Thanks, Damon. For everything. I know it's your job to try and reform kids like me, but—"

"Just so you know," he interrupts. "It's not *just* a job to me. Remember that. Call me if you need anything. I mean it."

"I'm out," Lenny calls out once he collects his stuff from the van. "My bus'll be here soon."

"If you need a ride—" Damon begins.

"I'm cool." Lenny waves bye to everyone as he heads over to the bus stop to wait.

"That's it?" Trish calls out to him. "You spend four weeks with us and all you can give us is a backwards wave?"

Lenny, still walking, flips her the finger. "Sit on this and spin, Trish," he yells back.

Trish is yelling something snarky back at Lenny while Damon is trying to defuse the situation so it doesn't escalate into a huge profanity/yelling match in front of the community center. As we're all saying our good-byes, Damon gets an emergency call from one of the kids in the juvenile probation program. He leaves after making us promise that we'll all make sure to call him if we ever need him.

Maggie's mom pulls into the parking lot next and heads toward us. The look on her face when she realizes I've been on the Re-START trip with Maggie makes me wince. If I had any doubts about whether or not Maggie and I could ever see each other again, even casually, her mom's horrified expression says it all.

I'm not welcome near her daughter. Ever.

"Mom, I want to say good-bye to everyone. I'll be there in a minute," I hear Maggie say. Her mom throws me a warning glare.

Maggie hugs everyone in the group. Tears come to her eyes as the girls all promise to call and see each other before Maggie leaves for her year abroad.

She hugs Matt next. "Take care of yourself," she says. "And don't give up on Becca."

"Who's Becca?" I ask them.

"My ex." Matt shrugs. "We broke up before the trip, but I kinda, well, you know ... Maggie's been giving me advice."

So he's not into Maggie? I just wish I'd figured that out sooner.

Maggie kisses me on the cheek. "Well, I guess this is good-bye ... again."

I nod. "Don't forget to show those Spaniards that Maggie Armstrong is a force to be reckoned with."

"Right," she says, amused. When she steps back, I

shove my hands in my pockets for fear I'll reach out for her. From the look of us, you'd never know we slept in the same bed last night and made out like the world was going to end if we stopped.

"Just so you know," she says, "I'm okay with saying good-bye this time. Really, I feel like we both have closure. I think you should go back to Paradise, but I can't force you to go home if you don't want to."

Her mom beeps the horn, reminding us that reality is always just around the corner ready to slap us in the face.

I gesture to her mom's car and give her a small smile. "You better go."

She takes another step away, but doesn't turn her back to me. "Stay out of trouble, Caleb. I mean it."

I don't take my eyes off her as she gets into her mom's car and they drive away.

Regret tugs at me, but I ignore it. There are some things we can't change even if we want to.

Trish gets picked up by her parents, sister, and brother. After hearing Erin's story, Trish's mom had to take a tissue from her purse so her own makeup wouldn't run. After that, the entire family packed Erin up in their van. I think they might just adopt the silent, tattooed girl. Matt left right afterwards, when his big brother came to give him a lift.

Re-START is officially over. I guess it's time for me to figure out where to go next.

One thing is for sure—I need to get far away. This time

Chicago is too close. I wasn't joking when I told Maggie I was going to Arizona. Problem is, I have exactly twelve dollars and sixty-three cents to my name. I can work odd jobs, construction day jobs if I can find them, until I can save up enough money to get me out of Illinois.

I swing my duffle over my shoulder, glad I have at least a few bucks to my name. I know of a cheap campground a few miles from here where I can stay a couple of nights while I figure out if there are any temporary jobs I can take to make some quick cash. I'll need at least a few hundred to get me a one-way bus ticket to Arizona.

"Hey, Caleb, wait up!"

I turn to find Lenny jogging to catch up with me. "Miss your bus?" I ask.

"Nah." He shrugs. "I didn't really have a bus to catch. I was thinking of, you know ... going with you," he says, as if it was something we'd already discussed and agreed to.

Umm ... I don't think so.

"No, you're not. Go find out where Trish lives and follow her to her house."

"Are you kidding? The girl hates me."

"Maybe that's because you didn't wipe your pubes off the toilet."

I keep walking.

Lenny doesn't get the hint, and I'm starting to think he's serious about coming with because he continues to follow me.

"Come on, Caleb. Have a heart. Think of us as Fred

and Barney, Ben and Jerry, Thelma and Louise. You know you want to."

I stop walking and look right at Lenny. "Thelma and Louise died at the end of that chick flick."

"They died holding hands. Didn't it bring you to tears?"

"No."

"You still owe me a hug, remember?"

"No, I don't."

"So you're gonna leave me stranded here? What, afraid I'm gonna cramp your style?"

"I don't have a style, Lenny. Go home. You do have a home, don't you?" He doesn't answer. "You told Damon you were going home."

"I lied."

Shit. "If you haven't figured it out yet, I don't have a house to go to either. I'm going to a campground so I can at least have a place to do the four S's—shit, shower, shave, and sleep."

"Cool."

"There's nothing *cool* about it." I can tell Lenny's not letting up. He's like a damn stray dog that's following me. I glance at him. Normally he sports a cocky-ass expression, but not now. Now he looks worried, as if he's afraid I'm gonna ditch him and leave him alone.

I keep walking, feeling déjà vu. Maggie followed me off campus and look where that got me.

Lenny walks beside me. I don't tell him to back off, because I think the guy is scared to be left alone.

"Thanks, Caleb," he says after a while.

"Just... don't piss me off," I tell him.

"I won't. I promise."

It takes us almost an hour to walk to the Happy Camper Campground. I register and pay the lady in the office for a camping spot that costs me seven dollars a day. It would've cost me twenty-two if I required a water spout, but I can just go to the community bathroom for that.

No matter how cheap this place is, I've got to find some quick cash. Once the Illinois summer is over, winter creeps in fast and furious. I'll freeze my ass off and die if I don't head for Arizona by then.

When it's dark and we've bought a couple of hot dogs at the little on-site store, the family at the site next to us gives us a few pieces of their wood and fire starters. Gotta love the generosity of campers.

After I've washed up in the Happy Camper Campgrounds community bathroom/shower area, I pull out a light blanket I bought when I was living at Rio's place.

"Here," I say, handing it to Lenny. "We can switch off days we use it."

"I'm fine," he responds.

I watch as Lenny rolls one of his shirts up to make a pillow, then pulls out a pair of sweats from his duffle and puts it over his face, making a circle in the middle where his mouth is.

"Why the hell are you wearing pants on your head?" I ask. "You look ridiculous."

"I'm not risking getting sunburned or mosquito bites on my face again. I've got an extra pair of boxers if you want to cover your face. They're not washed, but—"

"No thanks." Just the thought makes me want to puke.

Thank God we got assigned a grassy campsite. I spread the blanket on the ground. A sleeping bag would be great, but I'm happy to have my little spot of land for the night without having to worry about getting busted by the cops or bothered by other homeless people.

"Really, Lenny, why are you here?" I ask. "I mean seriously, man, what's your story?"

"I don't got a story," Lenny says, lifting his pants off his face. "You heard me the past four weeks tell all the sordid details. I got drunk, stole a car, and drove it into a lake. End of story."

He turns his back to me and faces the opposite direction.

I stare up at the sky, the stars and moon lighting up the endless universe. Wherever Maggie is, whether she's in Paradise or in Spain, she'll be looking up at the same moon and same stars.

Will she ever think about me? Will she remember the night we spent in the castle or last night when we slept in each other's arms? Or will she only remember the times we argued and tried to push each other away, because it was easier than admitting or accepting what was really happening between us?

Damn. I better get a grip and forget about Maggie Armstrong. *This* is my life—here on this little seven-dollar rented piece of land … I look over at Lenny … *and it doesn't seem like my lot in life is gonna get better anytime soon.*

The biggest torture right now is knowing I won't sleep much. When it's all quiet and I'm just lying down at night, that's when my mind wanders to things I have no right thinking about.

"It was my mom's boyfriend's car," Lenny says, his voice cutting through the silence. He'd been so quiet the past hour I thought he was sleeping. I guess I should've known better, since he wasn't snoring. "He packed up and left her five years ago and I thought he was gone for good. I can't *believe* she took him back. Want to know what he did?"

"You don't have to tell me." I'm not one to pry into other people's business, 'cause I don't want them prying into mine.

I look over at Lenny, who's got his palms pressed to his eyes. I've never seen him so serious.

"When my mom wasn't home he used to touch me."

"Damn, Lenny. That's some serious shit."

"Tell me about it." Silence fills the air, and he doesn't say anything else for a while. "At first I didn't really get what was goin' on, as if my brain couldn't wrap around the reality of what was happening. I was only twelve when it started. By the time the asshole split, I just wanted to erase it from my mind and forget it ever happened. I didn't tell anyone. But when he showed up in March and my mom said she invited him to live with us, I freaked."

"Did you tell your mom about what he did to you?"

"Yeah, but she pretty much got pissed off and called me a liar. The first night the guy moved back in, I got drunk, stole his car, and drove it in the lake. My mom didn't even come to court. I hear she married the douche. Damon said I could join the Re-START program instead of serving probation time. I promised him I'd go back home and work things out with my mom, but that's never gonna happen. She chose to trust a boyfriend over her son."

"I don't even know what to say." Somehow Lenny's story makes me feel like all the stuff I've gone through is nothing.

"You don't need to say anything. I didn't tell you to get your pity."

"Does Damon know what the guy did to you?"

"Nah."

"You should've told him."

"Yeah, well you should've told your parents the truth about the night you *didn't* hit Maggie with your car, but you didn't have the guts."

A flash of regret makes me tense up. "You're right," I admit. "But I promised I'd keep quiet."

"Yeah, well, I made a promise to that scumbag that I'd never tell my mom what he did to me, but I didn't keep that promise. I don't have choices anymore, Caleb. I *can't* go back home. It'll be different for you."

"What are you saying?"

Lenny sits up. "I'm sayin' that you've got choices I don't have. Hell, just because your mom's got some prescription drug addiction and wants you to act all perfect and your old man's a pussy doesn't mean you have to give up on them." Lenny turns his back to me again. "If I were you—"

"Yeah, well you're not me," I cut in harshly.

I get up and walk around the campground, angry at myself and at Lenny and at Leah and at the world in general. I'm glad most people are sleeping and the place is quiet except for the crackling of fires and low whispers of the few campers still awake.

I circle the campground five times, thinking the entire time about what Lenny said. Indecision replaces my anger. As I start walking faster and faster, crazy thoughts run through my head. Soon I start running. The faster I run, the more my mind races with thoughts of what was and what could be. *No, I can't,* I tell myself. *But what if I did?*

I get back to my little piece of rented land and see Lenny lying there by himself, sleeping on the ground. It's like looking at myself from far away, and it's pathetic—*I'm* pathetic. I have tons of regrets, stemming from my fear of being rejected by people I care about.

I don't want to be alone. I don't want my family to think I gave up on them. I also don't want Maggie to think

I gave up on us. My mouth goes dry and my heart is racing as I realize what I'm going to go.

I'm going back to Paradise.

I'm going home.

TWENTY-FOUR

Maggie

"Mom, it was no big deal."

"How can you say that, Maggie? It's the biggest deal."

I've been sitting at our kitchen table for the past twenty minutes not being able to eat any of the lunch set in front of us because I'm too busy getting lectured by my mother about the dangers of being on the Re-START trip with Caleb. Last night she hardly talked to me. Now she's giving me a lecture.

"I'm appalled that the program coordinator allowed it to happen."

"Mom—"

"He could have hurt you."

"Mom—"

"If you think the Caleb Becker you saw on that trip is the same boy who lived next door to us when you were growing up, guess again."

"Mom—"

"How can I trust you to make the right choices when you're over four thousand miles away in Spain, Maggie? If you think it was okay to travel around the Midwest with *that boy*, what other irresponsible decisions are you going to make?" She picks up her fork and pokes her chicken breast. "To be honest, I hoped when he left, he was gone for good."

"He *is* gone for good, Mom," I tell her. "He didn't think he'd be welcome back in Paradise, and I told him he was wrong. I told him people would give him a chance and not judge him." I take my napkin off my lap and put it on the table. "I guess I was wrong."

"Why are you so rebellious all of a sudden?" she asks when I get up and grab my purse.

I sigh. "I'm not, Mom. I'm just frustrated. I love you, but sometimes you have to trust me."

"I can't. Not when it comes to Caleb. His family is still struggling to bounce back from the pain and suffering he caused *all* of us. You were the one physically hurt by his reckless stupidity. How can you protect him? Because he's a good-looking boy? There are plenty of them out there, honey. Trust me."

I can't listen anymore.

"I'll be back later," I say as I walk out of the kitchen. I

turn around before I leave and say, "I love you, Mom. You know that, right?"

"I do. I love you, too."

"Then trust me. I don't stick up for Caleb because he's good-looking. I stick up for him because he doesn't deserve all the bad things that have happened to him." I hold my hand up when I think she's going to cut me off. "He made a mistake. Mom, we all make mistakes. Don't we all deserve a second chance?"

I head for Mrs. Reynolds' house in the Cadillac she gave me in her will. I miss her so much. She was the person who urged me to forgive Caleb, and she was right. I didn't want to at first. Just looking at Caleb when he came back from jail made my pulse race and my body shiver with anxiety.

But then we talked. A lot. Before I realized he wasn't the one who hit me, I forgave him. And fell for him.

I pull up to the house, expecting it to be vacant. Lou, Mrs. Reynolds' son and my mom's boyfriend, is standing out front watering the grass. There's a *For Sale* sign out front.

When he sees me pull up, he smiles. "Hiya, Maggie," he says. "What brings you to this side of town?"

"I just wanted to check the daffodils out back," I tell him.

"Some are still blooming. I've been trying to sell this place for months now, without a bite. Market is dead out here, so I'm probably not going to be able to sell it anytime soon." He sighs. I know he grew up in this house and it has sentimental value. His mom, Mrs. Reynolds, is gone, but her spirit is still here. "Where's your mom?" he asks.

"At home." I guess I should let him know about the drama back home. "She got mad because I never told her Caleb had joined the Re-START trip."

"She called me about that a few hours ago," he tells me. "Care to talk about it?"

"I guess." We walk to the backyard, side by side. My dad never walked with me anywhere. He was too busy going out of town for work or watching television. He didn't have an interest in me, or my mom. I used to pray he'd come back. The last time we talked was months ago. He said he'd come see me graduate from high school, but he never did.

I didn't even get a congratulatory call on graduation day.

I stop thinking about my dad when I catch sight of the gardens in the backyard. I'm surprised to see the daffodils are still thriving, the bright rainbow of colors immediately raising my spirits. It's breathtaking.

If Mrs. Reynolds were alive, she'd love them. She gave me meticulous directions on how to plant each bulb even though she knew she was dying and would never see them come up to display themselves with such radiance and, strangely enough, pride. Each variety seems to have an attitude all its own.

I wish Caleb were here to see them. He made the gazebo while I planted the daffodil bulbs, both of us slaving away to please Mrs. Reynolds.

"My mom's mad that I didn't quit the trip when I found out Caleb was on it," I tell Lou.

"You have to admit she has reason to distrust him."

"I get it, but..." I don't know how much to tell him. If he finds out Caleb didn't hit me with the car, he'll have to tell my mom. If *she* knows, she'll try and find out who really did hit me. And the vicious cycle would repeat.

I don't want that to happen. Since Caleb won't be coming back to Paradise, it's not worth the havoc it would cause.

"It's not like he's coming back to Paradise. He's not."

Lou sits one of the rocking chairs his mother used to sit in. "How do you feel about that?"

"I don't know." I look over at Lou, rocking away. He reminds me of his mom. "We kinda got close on the trip. It was nice."

"Should I ask how close?"

"Probably not."

I sit in the rocking chair beside him. We rock for a while, neither of us talking. The fresh summer air is warm even as the sun moves lower in the sky.

Lou chuckles. "You know, my mother would be giving us a piece of her mind right now. She'd call us lazy, then she'd give us chores and wouldn't be satisfied until we were working and sweating our butts off."

"I loved her," I tell him. I try not to think about losing her too much, or I'll break down and cry. Mrs. Reynolds was a strong lady and wouldn't want me to cry for her. "Even when she made me work my butt off, I appreciated it. She was the first person after I got home from the hospital who didn't treat me as if I had a disability."

"She loved you, too. And I figure she liked Caleb," he says, gesturing toward the gazebo he knows Caleb built all by himself. He was assigned to work here to finish out his community service obligations. "My mom always said I shouldn't hold grudges. Said they'd ruin your life."

"I wish my mom felt the same way."

"Want me to talk to her about it?" he asks. "Maybe I can smooth the waters some."

I look at the guy who has not only been my mom's boss and the owner of Auntie Mae's diner, but also the only man who's made my mom smile again.

"That would be great."

"Your mom's a sweet woman. She's just protective of you."

"I know." I wipe away an invisible piece of lint as I look down at my jeans. I used to hate that Lou was dating my mom. But now I can't help but be thankful he's in her life. And mine. "I don't know if I've ever told you, but my mom's a new person since she started dating you. She needs you."

That makes him smile. He clears his throat and says, "I've been meaning to ask you this for a while now, but I didn't gather up enough nerve before you left for the Re-START program and now that you're here..."

He clears his throat again.

"I'd like to ask your mother to marry me. Would that be okay with you, Maggie?"

TWENTY-FIVE

Caleb

I walk toward my house, the biggest one on the entire block. Maggie's house, next door, is practically dwarfed by ours.

I follow the brick sidewalk that my dad and I laid three years ago up to the front door. My house looks familiar and yet ... in some ways totally foreign to me. I notice the paint peeling off of the wood trim. One of the gutters is falling off, and no flowers have been planted out front. My mom used to plant them every summer. She said it made our house look like a home.

She was right.

I take a deep breath and focus on the front door.

How do you come back home after running away? If I

open the door and just walk in like I used to, they'll think I'm an intruder. A stranger.

Will they treat me like one once they take a look at me?

I look back down the street, wondering if I should retreat and forget coming home. I can just retrace my steps and disappear again. Nobody would know, and it would be easier than dealing with the drama about to unfold. But disappearing would be the coward's way out.

I'm not a coward.

Not anymore, at least.

I put my duffle down and ring the doorbell. My pulse is racing a billion times a second, like I just ran a marathon. Different scenarios about how my parents and sister will react are flying through my head.

I hear footsteps. Is it my mom, dad, or Leah? I don't have time to think about it too long because the door opens and my sister is standing in front of me.

My twin sister.

The one I went to jail for. She's still got dyed-black hair, light brown at the roots, but her clothes aren't as freaky as when I left. Instead of chains dripping off her jeans, she's wearing normal jeans. Her shirt is black to match her hair.

The last time I saw her she looked like death. Her hair was black, her nails were black, and her mood matched her black clothes. It freaked me out at first, but then it pissed me off. I was the one who went to jail so she'd live an easy life at home. How dare she become a recluse and change her appearance and attitude and live like the dead? She had no right...

At least her nails aren't black, and she's not wearing black eyeliner and black lipstick. It's a big improvement.

My throat goes dry at the same time tears flood her eyes.

"Caleb," she squeaks out. "You came back."

"For a little while, at least," I manage to say.

When I came home from jail, Leah had catapulted herself into my arms and hugged me tight. Not this time. She's definitely keeping her distance. Does she think I'm a ghost or that I'll suddenly disappear if she gets close?

"Maggie said she was going to urge you to come home, but I didn't believe her." Her hands are stiff at her sides. "I can't believe you're here."

"Well, believe it." I crane my head to see if there's anyone else home. "Yeah, so, uh... can I come in?"

She opens the door wider and steps back. "Yeah," she says slowly. "Umm, Dad's not home."

"Where is he?" I ask as I step into the foyer.

Leah starts biting on one of her fingernails nervously. "He went to visit Mom."

"*Visit* Mom? She's in rehab right now?" Oh, hell. Maybe it's worse than I thought.

"She's been there awhile. It's not her first time."

I let out a slow breath. "All right." I can deal with this, but... "Anything else I need to know about?"

"Like what?"

"I don't know, Leah." I'm on edge and want answers. Will she give them to me? "Is Dad coping with things okay? What's *your* story these days?" Man, why did I say that? I don't want to confront her when I haven't even been back for five minutes. "Forget I asked that last part."

Leah opens her mouth to say something, then closes it.

"I invited a friend to stay over," I say.

"Who?"

"His name's Lenny. If a guy who needs a haircut and wears a green T-shirt that says *I'm Your Daddy* rings the doorbell, assume it's him." I couldn't leave Lenny out on the streets. When he isn't trying his best to be a complete asshole, he's not so repulsive. He even insisted on giving me a couple hours to get reacquainted with my family before he came in.

I take my duffle and head up the stairs.

"Where are you going?" Leah asks, her voice clearly in a panic.

"To my room."

"Wait!" Leah yells, but it's too late.

I open the door to my room. Or what used to be my room. It's been turned into an office. No bed, no curtains, no closet full of clothes. Wow, they even got rid of my trophies. No sign of me anywhere.

In eight months all evidence of my life has been erased.

I have a feeling coming back here was the biggest mistake of my life.

TWENTY-SIX

Maggie

My mom is getting married. Well, she will be getting married after Lou proposes to her sometime this weekend.

I pull out some stationery and head over to Paradise Park. I want to write a letter to Vanessa. I don't want her to think I forgot about my promise to write her.

I sit leaning against the big tree at the park where Caleb and I first kissed. I feel at peace right here, and wonder if Caleb is doing okay in Arizona or wherever he is.

I write about the Re-START trip, and I tell Vanessa about Lou asking my permission to marry my mom. I thought I'd write a small note, but I end up getting carried away. I tell her about Caleb and Trish and Lenny ... by the time I'm done I've filled out the front and back of three pages.

When I get back home, Matt calls. He's really nervous about seeing his girlfriend again.

"I need you as a buffer," Matt says. "Becca agreed to go out with me tomorrow night. I need you there."

"I'm not gonna be a third wheel, Matt." That's the last thing I want.

"Things with Becca have been strained since the accident. I know you two will get along. Just … come on, Maggie. You need to help me break the ice. Pleeease. I know you're not leaving for Spain for another couple of weeks. What else are you doing besides sulking about Caleb?"

"I'm not sulking."

He laughs. "Okay, what have you done since coming back home from Re-START?"

"I unpacked."

"And … ? You've been home almost a week."

"And went to see Mrs. Reynolds' daffodils."

"Sounds like a blast so far. And?"

"And I just wrote a letter."

Matt laughs again. "Yeah, I see you have the most exciting life. I'm surprised you have time to talk to me on the phone."

Okay, so maybe Matt's right. I should go out with him and Becca tomorrow, and prove to myself that I'm not living in the past.

"Okay, fine," I tell Matt. "But who am I going to find to go out with me?"

"I've got an idea."

"Oh, no. I feel a headache coming on."

"Be adventurous," Matt says, now totally excited. "I'll find you a date. Just give me your address and be ready to go out tomorrow night at six."

After I hang up, I go to my room. There's a note on my bed. It's from my mom, telling me that my dad called and wants to talk to me.

I crumple up the piece of paper, toss it in the trash, and sit on my bed staring at the garbage can. What's so important that he wants to talk to me now?

I used to call and practically beg for five minutes of his time. I begged him to come back home, but he said he'd moved on. Why should I give him the time of day now? He doesn't deserve it.

If he plans to tell me his new wife is pregnant, does he expect me to jump up and down? Am I a bad person for resenting his new wife and his new life without me? He never once invited me to Texas to visit him. He shut me and my mom out in the same breath.

But what if he's sick? What if it's not that he's having a kid, but that he's got cancer or some other incurable condition? I hate my dad, but I still love him. I know that doesn't make sense, but then again, nothing in my life makes sense lately.

I feel like a hypocrite telling my mom to give Caleb

another chance when I'm unwilling to give my father another chance.

I pick up my phone and dial my father's number. I hold my breath each time the phone rings.

"Sweetheart, is that you?"

I feel numb when I hear his voice. Not excited, not angry, not anxiety-ridden. Just numb. "Yeah, it's me. Mom said you called."

I wait for the big news he needs to tell me.

"I've been trying to reach you for weeks. I have news," he says, then pauses.

I brace myself for it. Here it comes...

"I'm getting divorced," he blurts out.

Whoa, I didn't expect to hear that. "Sorry."

"Don't be. Sometimes these things work out, and sometimes they don't. You want to know the best part?"

I'm taken aback by his nonchalant attitude. "The best part?" I echo.

"I'm moving back in with you and Mom."

What?

No.

It's a mistake.

I must have heard him wrong. "You're moving back here? In our house?"

"I knew you'd be excited."

"Does Mom know?"

He gives a nervous laugh. "Of course she knows, silly. Isn't it great news, Maggie? We'll be a family again."

"Yeah," I say without emotion. I'm stunned, and I feel like my entire world has just tilted on its axis. "That's, umm … great."

"I'll be flying in on Thursday, and the movers are coming on Friday to move my stuff back in. I've got to get packing and wrapping things up here, so I'll see you next week. Bye, sweetheart."

As usual, he hangs up before I say bye back.

I wait impatiently until my mom gets home at six. Before she can take her waitress uniform off, I corner her in the hall.

"Why are you letting Dad come live here?"

"You called him," she says, stating the obvious. She slowly takes off her apron and drapes it over her arm. "Because he's getting divorced and wants to try again."

"So you're letting him? He left us, Mom. He left us and didn't look back."

"He's looking back now."

I want to give my dad a second chance, but then realize he's had many chances to come back and hasn't. I get a sinking feeling he'll only stay here until something better comes along.

"What about Lou?"

She starts up the stairs. "Lou is great, but he's not your dad. You always said you wanted to be a family again, Maggie. Your dad is the man I married."

"He's the man who divorced you. And replaced you."

She turns around and waves a finger at me. "Don't disrespect me. Your father made a mistake. He wants to make things right."

Tears well in my eyes. "Lou has been more of a dad than my own flesh and blood. He makes you happy. He makes us happy. I don't understand, Mom. It just doesn't make sense."

She stops when she reaches the top of the stairs. "I broke up with Lou tonight. I told him about your father coming back. It's over."

This can't be happening. Just when things were going right, they're all going wrong. I press my hands to my eyes, trying to shut out the world. But it's not about me. It's about my mom.

I hobble as fast as I can up the stairs and envelop her in a big hug. I start to cry. "I just want you to be happy, Mom."

She hugs me back and squeezes me tight. She's crying, too. "I want you to be happy, too."

We stand here, crying and holding each other for what seems like forever. We're two women who've been left to fend for ourselves for a long time now. When the doorbell rings, it startles both of us.

My mom wipes her eyes with the skirt of her uniform and heads back downstairs to open the door.

"Lou!" she says, startled.

Lou is holding a huge bouquet of red roses in one hand and a ring box in the other. He kneels on the porch, and I notice his eyes are bloodshot and puffy as if he's been crying.

"Marry me, Linda." He opens the ring box and takes my mom's hand gently in his. "Please tell me I'm not too late."

TWENTY–SEVEN

Caleb

Leah, Lenny, and I are sitting in my parents' living room, waiting for my dad to come home. Leah's got her fingers folded neatly in her lap and Lenny is looking at her with one cocked eyebrow. I drilled him endlessly before we came here, making sure I had his word that he wouldn't talk about the accident or the fact that he knows I wasn't the one who really hit Maggie.

"So, Leah," Lenny says as he looks across the room at Leah with one eyebrow cocked. "You got a boyfriend?"

I whack Lenny on the chest with the back of my hand. "What're you doing?"

He looks at me as if *I'm* the crazy one. "Makin' conversation, Caleb. Someone around here has got to fill the dead air. Neither of you is doin' such a bang-up job at it."

"You don't have to fill the air with bullshit," I tell him.

Lenny rolls his eyes. "Okay, Mr. Crabbypants."

"Didn't anyone ever tell you to talk only if you have something to—"

"No," Leah interrupts, her voice almost a whisper.

Lenny and I both look at my sister.

She looks down at the carpeting. "I meant no, I, uh, don't have a boyfriend."

Lenny leans forward. "Why not?"

She shrugs.

"Maybe if you smiled it would help."

What is this, the Lenny Self-Help Show? "Seriously, man, shut the fuck up. What do you know about girls, anyway? You're in love with Trish and all you can do is piss her off and dump her in a lake. You don't know shit about girls."

"And you do?" Lenny laughs. His stupid long hair falls in his eyes and he flicks it back. "I got one word for you, Mr. Crabbypants—Maggie."

At the mention of Maggie, my sister's eyes meet mine. I bet we're both thinking about our little deception that messed up both our lives.

"I'm going to get some water," Leah mumbles, then scurries away.

As soon as she disappears, the door opens. I stand, stiff at attention, as my dad walks through the front door.

He's wearing a suit, carrying the briefcase he's had for the past ten years, and sporting the same mustache he's had for the past twenty years.

When he sees me, his expression goes from blank to shocked. He freezes in his tracks.

"Hey, Dad," I manage to say.

"Caleb."

I walk toward him, not knowing if I should hug him or shake his hand or pat him on the back or … do nothing. It's sad when your own father has become a stranger.

I stop in front of him. He's still holding his briefcase and staring at me. What do I say to him now?

I blurt out, "I know I should have probably called and told you I was coming, but—"

"We haven't heard from you in months, Caleb."

"I know. I couldn't stay here anymore, Dad. Not like the way things were."

"Your mother is sick," he tells me. "She's been in the hospital on and off for months now."

He says it as if she has a terminal disease. I bet calling her "sick" is the standard excuse he's decided to use instead of saying "she's in rehab" or "she's a drug addict."

"I know."

I step back, realizing this isn't going to be a joyous reunion where my father welcomes me back with open arms. I should have had a clue that's the way it was going to be when I saw my room had been converted to an office and all signs I'd ever existed had vanished.

He's holding his briefcase in front of him, almost like a barrier between us. "We didn't know if you were dead or alive. Your mother had to make up a story."

I shouldn't be surprised. My mom is the queen of making up stories to make our family look good. "What did she say?"

"She said we sent you to an exclusive boarding school in Connecticut."

A hearty, snorting laugh comes from the couch. Or, to be exact, it comes from Lenny who's sitting on the couch.

"Who's that?" my dad asks.

"Lenny."

Lenny springs off the couch and envelops my dad in a huge bear hug. My dad steps back, totally caught off guard, but keeps his balance. I bet he's silently thanking his high school football coach for those balance drills in high school.

"Nice to meet you, Dad," Lenny says. "Or should I call you Dr. Becker? Or Dr. B., or just Doc?"

I push Lenny off my dad. "Lenny's kind of a friend of mine," I tell my dad. "More like a sidekick."

I figure that's better than explaining that Lenny is a delinquent who thinks he's funny and doesn't have a filter when it comes to his mouth.

My dad puts his briefcase in the hall closet and says to Lenny, "You can call me Dennis."

"Cool. Give me a fist bump, Dennis." Lenny holds out his fist mid-air and waits for my dad to do the same.

My dad doesn't. I'm not sure he's ever given anyone

a fist bump. It's not that my dad is stupid or old fashioned. He's just…proper. He doesn't stray from the norm, because he likes his life neat and tidy.

Me being home is messing up his tidy life.

I'm sure it's killing him that my mom is in rehab. He probably doesn't know what to do about it, and there's no rule book or game plan when it comes to the grim realities of our lives.

"Are you guys, uh, in town for a while?" Dad asks me. "Or are you just passing through?"

It's a question you'd ask an acquaintance, not your son.

Leah is leaning against the stairs, waiting intently for my answer.

I'm tempted to say I'm just passing through. It would be easier than telling the truth, that Lenny's story made me realize I need to come back and make peace with my family.

"I was thinking of staying for a few weeks," I mumble.

"At a hotel, or…" Dad's voice trails off.

"I was hoping to stay here, Dad."

Lenny sticks his chin on my shoulder. "Me too, Dennis."

My dad scratches his head. "Umm…I guess, umm… we don't really have beds to spare. We turned your room into an office."

"I'll sleep on the couch," I tell him, feeling like I'm begging for a place to stay in my own house. It doesn't sit well in my gut.

"I'll sleep on the floor," Lenny chimes in, apparently having no problems begging. "Unless you want me to sleep in bed with Leah." Lenny holds his hands up when all of our heads snap up at his last comment. "Just kidding."

My sister steps forward and says, "I'll go get some sheets and blankets from the hall closet."

"Okay," my dad says. "But you boys better keep the house clean. My wife hates a messy house."

"Got it," I tell him, wondering if I need to remind him that "his wife" is my mom. And that she's in rehab, not here.

The loud sound of Lenny clapping his hands together makes us all turn to him. "Now that that's settled, what's for dinner?"

"Maybe we should order in some pizza," Dad says as he walks upstairs. He always changes into jeans and a T-shirt after work. It's his ritual.

When my sister and dad are out of hearing range, I let out a slow breath.

I'm home.

It doesn't feel like home, though. I wonder if I'd get a better reception if I showed up at Maggie's house. Who am I kidding? Her mom would toss me out or call the cops to have me thrown back in jail.

"Your dad is one weird dude," Lenny says. "But I like him."

At dinner, when Lenny excuses himself to go to the bathroom, I ask, "So, can I go see Mom?"

My dad puts down his pizza. "I don't think so, Caleb."

"Why not?"

"Because she's fragile. I'm not sure she could handle it right now."

"I'm her *son*," I say through clenched teeth.

"After you left, she said you were dead to her."

I look to my sister for confirmation, but she's staring at her plate. Anger starts to fire up in my veins. "Leah!"

She looks up. "What?"

What? All she can say is *what*?

I stand, my chair scraping the floor. "Thanks a lot, Leah," I grind out. "Thanks a lot for *nothing*."

TWENTY-EIGHT

Maggie

I peek into my mom's room as I'm getting ready for the double date. She's sitting on her bed, staring at the open box with the ring Lou gave her still inside. She didn't say yes to him when he came over last night and proposed, but she didn't say no.

She said she needed time to think.

She's definitely thinking.

"Did you tell Dad about Lou?" I ask her.

"I called him today," she says, her voice sad and wistful.

"And?"

"And...I don't know," she says, then shrugs. "I'm confused. I thought I knew what I wanted, but when Lou came by last night he got me thinking, and now...now I'm just confused."

I sit on the bed next to her and smile. She brushes the hair out of my face and sighs. "I thought for so long that if your dad came back, it would make our lives whole again."

"I know. I did, too. Until Lou came along."

"But he's not your dad. I fell in love with your dad first, and I don't know if I can give Lou as much of myself as I gave your father."

"He loves you, Mom."

"I know. But is it enough?"

"That's for you to decide. I'll support you, no matter what you choose."

"I just thought...well, forget it. Don't think about anything except having fun. I'm glad you're going out."

"Me too." I hadn't been looking forward to tonight, but when I took a shower and started getting ready, I got excited. Well, not excited for my mystery date, but excited to be doing what I said I was doing—moving on with my life.

Sometimes moving on takes effort.

Sometimes moving on is harder than it looks.

Going out is the first step to Maggie Armstrong moving on in life. I may have a limp, but that doesn't mean my social life or dating life has to be dead.

I take a deep breath and tell myself, *it is what it is*. I can't turn back the clock and undo the accident. It happened. This is who I am now, take it or leave it.

But when I look at my clock and notice it's five forty-five, I have second thoughts. I don't know if I'm ready to move on. I can't imagine myself kissing anyone besides Caleb. I know that's ridiculous, but right now it's true.

At five after six, as I'm ready to bite my fingernails to the core with anticipation and anxiety, the doorbell rings.

I plaster a smile on my face and open the front door. Standing in front of me is Matt, a girl with short spiky blonde hair, and...

"No way!" I say with a smile.

My physical therapist, Robert, opens his arms wide. "You didn't think I'd let you leave for Spain without one last goodbye, did you?"

I narrow my eyes at Matt. "Did you have this planned all along?" I ask him, as Robert hugs me like a brother.

"Yeah. So shoot me if we wanted to surprise you. Becca, this is Maggie. Maggie, Becca." While I greet Matt's girlfriend, Matt nudges Robert. "Maggie even put on makeup for you. I've never even seen her with makeup on."

My mom comes in the foyer, pretending she was just passing through on her way upstairs instead of having it all timed so that she could meet my "date."

"Robert?" she says, confused.

Robert, wearing a fashionable brown sports jacket to match his fashionable glasses says, "I couldn't let Maggie leave for an entire year without a goodbye celebration. She's my date tonight."

My mom has known Robert for almost two years now,

ever since he came to the hospital after my surgery and was assigned to be my personal torture instructor ... I mean physical therapist. I used to fantasize about pulling his perfectly spiked hair right out of his head when he wouldn't give up on me and I desperately wanted him to.

More times than not, I cried in front of him. I hated when Robert expected me to push myself to the limit. When I thought I couldn't bend my leg any more, Robert would make me go one step further.

I didn't appreciate him at the time, that's for sure. It took us a while to become friends. I was actually entertained by all of his stories about dating girls. Robert is a self-proclaimed bachelor and says he'll never settle down because he gets bored easily when it comes to girls. He says just like he can't eat Chinese food every day, he can't date the same girl without getting the itch to find someone different.

I once told him he'd die a very lonely man, and his good looks would one day fade, but he didn't seem worried. The guy has way too much confidence, but I wouldn't trade him for anything.

After my mom hugs Robert and meets Matt and Becca, she says, "You kids stay out at long as you want. Just have fun."

We decide to go to Dusty's Sports Bar & Grill. They serve food in the restaurant, so as long as you don't drink, you can be there if you're under twenty-one. Robert is already twenty-four, and he orders a beer while the rest of us order sodas.

It's nice that my first real date is a nondate, so I don't have to obsess over whether or not my disability is going to be an issue.

"Maggie, have you been doing the stretching exercises we'd discussed before you went on your trip this summer?" Robert asks.

I take a fry from the basket we'd ordered and dip it in some ketchup. "Can I lie?"

Matt, Becca, and I all laugh while Robert shakes his head. It feels good to go out and get my mind off of Caleb. I feel like every minute my mind isn't occupied, it wanders to thoughts of him.

Like now. While I'm having a good time, way better than I expected, I wonder if Caleb would have his arm around me like Matt has his arm draped around Becca, if we were on a date. And the way she looks up at him reminds me of—

"I bet you've been stiff," Robert says.

Right. Back to the here and now. *Stop thinking about Caleb.*

I roll my eyes. "You're off duty. Remember, you're supposed to be my date tonight, not my therapist." My fingers make quotation marks in the air when I say the word "date."

"She did complain of stiffness on the trip," Matt chimes in. He holds his hands up when I mumble *traitor.* "I'm just sayin'."

Robert moves his chair back and says, "Give me your leg, Maggie."

I blow out a frustrated breath and rest my leg on his knee. "It's fine. I'm fine."

"Flex for me."

I look over at Matt and Becca across the table as I flex. "Better you than me," Matt says, chuckling.

"Do you give a physical exam to all your dates?" I ask Robert as he cradles my jean-covered calf in his hand and watches how far I flex.

"No." He winks at me. "It's a first for me."

If it were any other guy, that wink would be cheesy, but I bet Robert practiced it in front of the mirror until it looked cool.

I cock an eyebrow and say, "I don't fall for your charms."

"Really? Wait, let me try it again." He winks a second time.

"Nope, doesn't do it for me. Besides, it's *really* inappropriate," I tell him, totally joking and he knows it. He's given me such a hard time in the past, I feel it's only fair for me to return the favor. "I'm your patient."

"Not anymore, you're not. You quit physical therapy. You're fair game."

"Ugh, you're too old."

"I'm twenty-four. How can that be too old?"

"I think you have some gray hair, Robert."

Robert's mouth goes wide and his hand cups his perfect head of hair. "I. Do. Not."

"Umm, Maggie," Matt says, then coughs a bunch of times. "I think the guy you really want just walked through the door."

TWENTY-NINE

Caleb

I'm trying to act like seeing Maggie with another guy is no big deal. I've wanted to call her since I came back. I should have called her. I didn't, and now she's out with a guy. She's got her leg resting on his knee, her calf cradled in his slimy hand.

What the fuck?

Does the dude know that a week ago she was lying in bed with me?

When Maggie looks my way, she whisks her leg off the guy's lap.

"Maggie! Matt!" Lenny practically yells across the bar. He's standing next to me, waving his arms as if he's on a desert island attempting to flag down a passing ship. Nobody's missing his presence, that's for damn sure.

Matt motions us over.

He shakes my hand when I reach their table. "Caleb and Lenny, this is my girlfriend Becca and that's Robert, our physical therapist."

Robert holds out his hand and shakes mine, then Lenny's. I give him a strong, hard shake so he knows I'm not a dead fish. The guy is drinking beer, and he looks like he came out of a damn *GQ* magazine spread. Is that the kind of guy she's looking for, an older one who wears fancy clothes?

"What are you doing here?" Maggie asks, totally confused.

"I came back."

"Have you seen Leah and your dad?"

"I'm staying with them." I pause. "For now. Lenny had some issues with his mom, so he's staying at my house too."

I'm trying to read her, but I can't. The guy she's with seems amused that I'm here. Has she told him about me? Does she even give a shit that I'm back, or was all that talk about coming back to Paradise solely for my parents' and sister's sake?

"Why don't you guys join us?" Robert asks.

Nice way to shove it in my face, dude. He has no clue if he attempts to stick his tongue down Maggie's throat in my presence, I'll be on him like a pit bull. "No, thanks."

Lenny spots an empty booth across the way and heads over to it.

"We'll talk later," I tell Maggie. I follow Lenny and slide into the booth.

As if the night couldn't get worse, my old high school friends walk through the door. I spot my old best friend Brian Newcomb right away, the guy who was dating Kendra while I was still dating her. She was sleeping with both of us and I had no clue. Brian knew, but he was too chickenshit to tell me about it.

He's with Tristan and Drew. The four of us were on the wrestling team together. We'd hung out since grade school. After I was released from jail, Drew was a cocky asshole and Tristan's mom ordered me to stay away from him. Tristan didn't argue.

I try not to make eye contact with the guys, and instead attempt to concentrate on whatever nonsense is flying out of Lenny's mouth. I think he's reminiscing about tossing Trish in the lake, but I'm hardly listening, because out of the corner of my eye I see Brian walking toward us.

"Holy shit, it really is you," Brian says, leaning into the booth and slapping me on the back. "Where you been, man?"

I try to fight off the feeling of camaraderie with Brian, but I can't. We were best friends for too damn long for me to turn my back and pretend he doesn't exist.

"I was in Chicago for a while," I tell him. Brian nods as if he understands. I gesture to Lenny. "This is Lenny. Lenny, these are my old friends."

"Cool." Lenny nods at each of them.

"Hey, Caleb," Tristan says, shaking my hand. "You're back, huh?"

"Just for a little while," I tell him.

Drew has a sly grin on his face as he sits on the bench beside me. "Brian, give Caleb the good news."

If Brian tells me he got a wrestling scholarship to Notre Dame, I won't be surprised. He always wanted to be one of the Fighting Irish, even though he's German. It was one of our running jokes. Brian is a smart guy, and worked hard to get the grades so he could get in.

Brian shoves his hands in his pockets. "Yeah, umm, I'm getting married."

"To *Kendra*," Drew chimes in, as if he can't keep the salacious info off his tongue. Drew hates Kendra, but he loves gossip that's sure to ignite sparks between Brian and me.

He's not going to get those sparks, at least from me.

I reach past Drew and hold out my hand to Brian. "Congrats, man," I say. And I mean it. I thought he'd go the college route, but if this is what he wants, more power to him.

Brian shakes my hand. "Thanks, Caleb. That's really cool of you."

I nod, and I'm glad that's over. The ice is broken. Tristan slides in next to Lenny, and Brian pulls up a chair to sit on the end.

This is one cozy little group.

Speaking of cozy little groups … I peer over at Maggie. She's having all sorts of fun with Matt, that guy Robert, and Becca. Okay, well not exactly *fun*. They're all just talking. I shouldn't give a shit. I don't give a shit.

How old is that dude, anyway? He's got a sports coat on as if he's about to broadcast the five o'clock news, and he's drinking his beer out of a glass instead of a bottle. The dude is a diva.

"So when's the wedding?" Lenny asks Brian.

"In two weeks," Brian mumbles as the waitress comes over.

After we order, Brian pulls out his cell phone and starts texting. For a guy who's getting married in two weeks, he doesn't look happy. In fact, he looks downright depressed.

I wouldn't put it past Kendra to manipulate him into marrying her, except for the fact that ever since sophomore year, Kendra has been obsessed with leaving Paradise and moving to California. She always wanted to be an actress or model and used to make fun of the people who graduated from Paradise High and stayed here their entire lives. She called them white trash losers.

Tristan tries to grab Brian's phone, but he pulls it out of his reach. "Stop it," he orders.

Our food comes, and I have to say thank God for Lenny. I don't feel like talking much, and Lenny can carry on a conversation about anything. When Lenny finds out Drew is into sports cars, he pulls all this random sports car knowledge out of his ass. Funny thing is, he sounds like he really knows what he's talking about.

When Tristan mentions the new Frisbee course that went up at the south end of Paradise Park, Lenny says he "loves frolfing" and that "technically it's called disc golfing because Frisbee is a brand name, yadda yadda."

Who knew Lenny was an encyclopedia of useless information? I'm just glad I don't have to carry the conversation, especially because I keep looking over at Maggie.

Oh, shit. I catch her looking back. Our eyes lock on one another.

"I've got to go," Brian says.

"Sit down, Bri," Drew says. "I drove you, remember? I'm not goin' anywhere until I finish my food."

Brian reaches into his wallet and tosses a ten dollar bill on the table. "You don't have to interrupt your meal, Drew. Kendra is picking me up."

Brian keeps looking at the door and holding his cell phone in his palm, as if he's expecting to be summoned by text any minute. Something's not right.

Apparently Kendra decides to come in rather than just text him, because she walks through the door and heads toward us. Her big blue eyes are focused on me and her long blonde hair is perfectly styled. Her makeup makes her look hard, not like the pretty girl I started dating when we were sophomores. She was my first serious girlfriend, and the one who I lost my virginity to. I used to think she was the sexiest thing alive.

"I thought you were going to text me when you got here," Brian says.

Kendra doesn't break her eye contact with me. "I had to see if it was true." She wets her top lip and throws me one of her all-too-familiar sexy looks. "So ... Caleb Becker is back. Again."

"Hey, Kend," I say. "I hear congratulations are in order."

She looks down at her ring finger and the small diamond. "Thanks."

"You ready?" Brian asks, taking her hand.

Kendra removes her hand from Brian's grasp. "Can I talk to CB outside for a minute?"

I haven't heard that nickname in a long time. CB, my initials. She always called me that.

Brian looks at me, then back at her. "Yeah, I guess so. But I thought you said we were late for the cake tasting."

"It's fine," is her response. "I need to talk to Caleb first."

Drew rolls his eyes, but slides out of the booth to let me out.

"We'll be right back," Kendra tells Brian. "Wait here."

She heads for the exit, and doesn't stop until we're next to the gravel parking lot.

"I can't believe you came back," she says.

I tell her the truth. "I needed to tie up some loose ends."

"Am I a loose end, CB? 'Cause I swear, all I've done since you left is think about you and me. Do you think about me?"

I'm confused. Why is she bringing us up when she was the one who cheated on me? "Why are you marrying Brian? 'Cause neither one of you look happy about it. I know for a fact that after graduation you were dying to leave this town and go out to California, and Brian was dead set on going to Notre Dame."

Kendra crosses her arms around her stomach. "I'm pregnant, Caleb."

Shit. Pregnant? Didn't see that coming, although I guess the evidence is right in front of my face. Kendra isn't wearing one of her signature tight shirts that hug her body. She's wearing a loose shirt with a light jacket.

Tears start welling in her eyes, making her eyelashes sparkle. When she blinks and black mascara falls down her cheek along with her tear, I don't know what to say.

"Sorry," I say dumbly.

"Brian doesn't even want to apply for college, Caleb. He wants to take over his dad's butcher shop. Can you imagine me staying in Paradise and being the wife of a butcher?"

She wraps her arms around my waist. I keep my hands off her, because damn it, I don't want Brian coming out here and thinking we're about to get it on. And I don't want Maggie seeing me with Kendra, either.

It was a bad idea coming out here with her. I take her wrists and unwrap her arms from around my waist.

"Kend...shit, why didn't you just use a condom or something? We were always careful."

"Yeah, well the next time a guy says he'll promise to pull out I'll remember that's not effective birth control."

She wraps her arms around me again. We dated for over two years, but she doesn't have a hold on me now.

I also know that Kendra can turn the damsel-in-distress act into the diva-with-an-agenda act in a matter of seconds.

She buries her head into my chest. "Take me with you," I think I hear her say.

"What?"

She looks up with wide blue eyes and blinks her long lashes.

"Take me back, CB," she says. "I never stopped loving you."

THIRTY

Maggie

I saw Kendra and Caleb leave the restaurant together, but I didn't expect to find them in an intimate embrace in the parking lot. As we walk out of Dusty's, I can't help but stare.

Kendra is looking up at Caleb. He's looking down at her.

Suddenly, I don't feel good.

If he bends his head further, they're going to kiss. I look down at the gravel. If he kisses her, I might have to hurl a rock at them.

Stop it, Maggie.

Okay, I need to get a grip. Caleb and I parted amicably. We're friends, above all else. And I'm glad he's finally back in Paradise, because I know his family needs him.

We get back to my house and hang out for a while, until Robert starts yawning and Matt drives him and Becca home. While I'm saying good-bye to them, Kendra drives up in her little sports car and parks in front of Caleb's house. She tosses her blonde hair back with a flick of her wrist. The pieces fall in perfect waves down the side of her face and land in little curls at the bottom.

She doesn't even look my way when she walks up to Caleb's door and rings his bell in all her sexy glory. I try not to pay attention as he opens the door and lets her in, but I can't help it. Old habits die hard.

After Matt drives off with Robert and Becca, I have the urge to ring Caleb's doorbell and fight for him like Lou is fighting for my mom.

Instead, I sit on our front steps and think. And wait. And wait.

What are you waiting for, Maggie? I ask myself.

I stand and go inside, feeling defiant. I get ready for bed, then peek outside. Kendra's car is still parked out front. Damn. I talk to my mom about my night, then peek outside again.

Sure enough, that sports car is still out front.

I toss and turn all night, resisting the urge to look out my window and check whether Kendra is staying the entire night.

Right now, I wish Caleb and I didn't live next door to each other.

In the morning, her car is gone. Caleb is sitting on his porch as I leave to go to the grocery store.

"Hi," I say curtly when he sees me.

"Hi," he says back.

I head toward my car. "Have a good night last night?"

"Yep. You?"

"The best. Robert's amazing."

"You trying to make me jealous?"

"Why? Are you jealous?"

"I didn't like his hands on you."

"He's my physical therapist," I say. "He just touched my leg."

Caleb jumps off his porch and heads my way. "Regardless, I still didn't like it."

I can't help but ask. "What *really* made you come back to Paradise? Was it Kendra?"

"No, it was Lenny, my parents, my sister." He shrugs. "You."

"Can we go for a walk?" I ask, putting my keys back in my purse. Without talking, we fall into step next to each other. Instinctively, we head for Paradise Park. "I was ready to let you go. I moved on."

"I know."

"And then I saw you hugging Kendra last night. When I saw her go into your house ... I've never felt more possessive in my life."

"Don't," he says. "She's marrying Brian in two weeks. They're engaged."

"I think she still wants to be with you."

"Well, that's not gonna happen. Nothing happened last night. We talked. That's it."

We stop when we get to the big oak tree. Caleb and I kissed here for the first time. I'll never forget how lonely and lost I felt until that kiss. It changed me.

He changed me.

Caleb looks up at the thick branches and green leaves waving at us from above. "This is our tree, you know."

"You used to climb it until you broke your arm when you fell off it. I watched you from afar back then." I give a short laugh. "I used to always watch you. I liked you for so long."

"Why?"

"Because you were popular and smart and cute and weren't afraid of anything or anyone. When Leah and I made you watch our dance shows, you pretended to be interested. You were selfless. When you took the blame for me breaking your mom's ceramic owl statue, you were my hero. I loved watching you, even if you didn't notice me then."

"And what about now?"

I sit on the ground with my back resting against the tree. "I still can't keep my eyes off of you. God, if my mom knew I was here with you admitting that fact, she'd freak out."

"You want to know what I realized last night?"

"That you miss having Kendra in your life?"

"No." He crouches on the ground, facing me. "I miss having *you* in my life. You're my best friend, Maggie. Call me crazy, but I want you to be my girlfriend—"

Oh, God, how I dreamed this day would come. But

it's too late, isn't it? I reach out and cup his beautiful face in my palm. "Caleb, I'm leaving in two weeks. I'll be gone for almost a year."

"I know. But we're here now, right?" He looks determined, as if he knows we can do this. "Why don't we test drive being a couple the next two weeks? Let's not think about what's gonna happen after that. What do you say, Maggie?"

THIRTY-ONE

Caleb

After I ask Maggie to be my girlfriend, she looks nervous. "What about your parents, my mom ... and Leah?" Her eyebrows are furrowed in worry.

Maggie and I are nothing like Kendra and Brian. I think my old best friend and my ex-girlfriend make each other weaker. Maggie and I, together, are one strong team.

"We're going to tell them about us."

Her eyes go wide. "Remember how upset they were last time? I can't."

"Maybe *you* can't, but together we can." I lean and kiss her on the lips. "Don't be afraid."

When I pull away, our eyes meet.

This is the girl I draw strength from. She's got more

power than she thinks, and she taught me the definition of resilience.

A slow smile crosses her lips. "You really think we can do this?"

"Yeah, I do." For the time being, I do.

In the evening, we decide to meet at the park after dark. Maggie's still nervous about telling people about us.

The moonlight glows on her beautiful face as she comes up to me. I sling my arm around her and we walk quietly. "What happens after I leave for Spain?" she finally asks.

Her trip does kind of throw a monkey wrench into the girlfriend plan. But can't we just live for today and not worry about the future? "I don't know. I guess we'll figure it out as we go along."

Maggie smacks her sweet lips together and holds her chin high. She looks ready for a challenge.

For the first time in forever, I feel like I can handle being in Paradise. I stroke her shoulder and slowly trail my fingers down her arm until our fingers touch. I love it when I touch her and hear her breathe harder and faster. It's a total turn-on. It makes me want to see just how much I can please her. "I wish we were back at the cabin right now."

"Me too," she whispers. "I'd make out with you all night."

I chuckle. "I got to be honest with you, Mags. I'd try to do a lot more than make out."

I like just being with Maggie, talking to Maggie, doing stuff with Maggie ... but I also like fooling around with Maggie. It drives me nuts that she doesn't realize how much sex appeal she's got.

That brings a shy smile to her face. "I like what we did at the cabin. It was hard to leave you in the morning."

"Tell me what you liked. You know, so I know for next time."

"I'm too embarrassed." I watch as she nibbles her lip, then cocks her head to the side, thinking. She turns to face me. "Um ... how about if I show you?"

This girl never ceases to amaze me. The more comfortable she is in our relationship, the more her feisty spirit comes out.

"Bring it on."

Without hesitation, she leans forward and brings her face right up to mine. Hoping nobody can see us, I grab her butt and back her up against the tree. "You okay?" I murmur.

"Mmm." Her legs instinctively go around me, and I press into her as she moans against my lips.

Damn, her kisses are hot and sexy. I feel her energy and eagerness as if it's my own.

I definitely don't have to wait long this time for her tongue to come out and play with mine.

When her soft hands reach under my shirt and toy with the waistband of my jeans, it feels so different than it has with any other girl. Sure, I lust after Maggie. But she makes me nervous, because I also love her. I love her for everything she is and wants to be. She challenges me to forgive others.

She's my best friend. That thought is humbling.

"Get a room," I hear a voice say from behind me.

Damn. One day Maggie and I are going to get some alone time even if I have to save up money to take her to Lake Geneva or Rockford for a weekend like my parents used to do.

I give a frustrated moan as I look over at the spawn of Satan, who can only be named Lenny. What I wasn't expecting was my old cellmate Julio to be standing beside him.

I gently release Maggie and stand in front of her. It's a sorry attempt at protecting her from Lenny's ridicule, but we're kind of caught in a compromising position.

"Hey, what're you doing here?" I ask Julio.

"Thought I'd pay you a little visit."

I assumed he'd go back to Chicago when he got released, to see his family and hang with old friends. I never really believed he'd come to see me.

Oh, man, what is Maggie going to think of Julio? I'm kind of glad it's dark, so she doesn't see all his tattoos. His shaved head makes him look like a badass, but his crazy tats are even more intimidating.

"Maggie, this is Julio. We shared a cell when I was in the DOC."

"Nice to meet you," Maggie says, holding out her hand and smiling.

Julio slaps her hand and shakes it like she's one of his homegirls. I'm amused that she doesn't seem fazed in the least. Julio nods at our obvious disheveled appearance. Maggie's hair is a mess from my fingers running through it, and I think she somehow managed to get my jeans unzipped without me even knowing. "Sorry to interrupt whatever you two were doin' ... or about to do."

As long as I've got an entourage, I might as well lay down the line. "Next time, if either of you catch me making out with my girlfriend, just pretend we don't exist and walk away."

"Girlfriend?" Lenny asks. "Since when did that become official?"

"Since just now," Maggie says.

"I can't imagine you came here just for a visit," I tell Julio.

Julio, as always, looks and acts cool. In his neighborhood, guys are afraid to screw around with guys who have swagger. You play the game and you don't get messed with.

"You know I don't like taking nothin' from nobody, but I need a place to stay."

If it was only up to me, no problem. Julio's not as crazy as he looks, and his being here is a sign he's breaking away from his gang ties. "I need to ask my dad. We'll work something out."

We walk to my house. The entire time I'm thinking about how I'm going to break the news to my dad that there's another friend of mine who needs a roof over his head.

Hell, I was just getting revved up to break the news

that Maggie and I are a couple. Now I have to deal with Julio needing a place to stay. I feel like an intruder or guest in my own house as it is. Bringing a second random guy to stay might cause my dad to freak out.

Maggie squeezes my hand. It's a silent message that everything will be okay. Somehow I believe her. In the end everything will be okay. But hurdles have to be jumped through first.

When we get to my house, I find my sister watching television in the living room. She looks surprised when all four of us walk in.

"Hi," she says as she clicks the television off. Her focus immediately goes to Julio.

"'Sup?" he says, nodding to her.

"Leah, this is Julio. Julio, Leah."

"Hi," she says.

"Where's Dad?" I ask her.

"He's either watching TV in his room, or sleeping."

I should have known. "Be right back," I tell everyone, then take the stairs two at a time and knock on my parent's bedroom door.

"Come in."

I open the door and find my dad lying on his big king-sized bed watching television. He turns it off when he sees me come into the room.

"Hey, Dad."

"Did you have a good time tonight?" he asks.

I think of Maggie and me. I don't know what the future

holds with us, but I feel good about it. I feel the best I've ever felt about us, actually. "Yeah. I had a great time, thanks. Listen, I've got to ask you a favor. This guy who I roomed with at juvie stopped by." I clear my throat, because I don't know how to proceed with asking for yet another favor from my dad. "He needs a place to crash."

"For how long?" Dad asks. I can't read his reaction, so I tread carefully. I'm at his mercy here. It's his house. Just before I left Paradise he'd said to follow his rules or leave. I left, because I couldn't pretend to be a perfect son when I clearly wasn't one.

"I don't know. A few days, maybe."

"We have valuables. Your mother wouldn't like it, Caleb."

"Mom isn't here," I tell him.

"What about Leah?" Dad says. "She's almost as fragile as your mother."

The floor creaks, alerting us there's someone else in the room. It's Leah.

"Let him stay, Dad."

"Why?"

"Because it's the right thing to do. He needs a roof over his head, and we have one." She looks at me and gives me a small smile, as if we're in this together.

"Fine. He can stay," he tells me. "Caleb, I'm holding you responsible if anything is stolen. And he can only stay a few nights and that's all. While your mother might not be here now, this is our home and I have to respect the way she'd want it to be."

"Thanks, Dad." I'm about to head back downstairs, but I need to get something off my chest first. I look at Leah, then my dad. "I just want both of you to know that Maggie and I are going to be spending a lot of time together the next two weeks."

"I don't think that's a great idea," my dad chimes in. "She's the reason you went to jail, Caleb."

I look right at my sister and say, "Maggie's not the reason I went to jail, Dad. Right, Leah?"

"I don't know what you're talking about," Leah mumbles. She retreats quickly and disappears down the hall.

"What are you thinking, Caleb?" my dad asks. "You're setting yourself up for trouble by messing around with Maggie. You're screwing up your life."

"You got it all wrong, Dad. I'm trying to fix it."

Maggie

I'm doing laundry in the morning when the doorbell rings. When I open the door, Caleb is standing on my porch with a steaming mug in his hands. "I made you coffee," he says, holding it out to me. "I forgot how you liked it, so I put in a little milk and sugar. If I had the money, I'd have gone out and gotten you gourmet stuff—"

"I don't need gourmet. You know that." I feel like everything is falling into place so perfectly, and it scares me. I take the cup and invite him in. "You didn't have to make me coffee at all."

"I wanted to. Besides, I figure we can talk to your mom and, you know, kind of break the news about us to her together."

"She's already at work," I tell him as I lead him to the laundry basket in the living room. "Sunday mornings tend to be busy at the diner."

I'm still not sure how my mom will react when she not only realizes that Caleb is back in Paradise, but that we're a couple now.

A couple.

I'm still trying to get used to the fact that we decided to make things official. It's so weird having him here, in my house, bringing me coffee just because he thought I'd want some.

"Did everything go okay last night after I left?" I ask as I pull out some T-shirts to fold.

He leans against the edge of the sofa, watching me. "I told my dad and Leah about us."

I stop folding and brace myself for the aftermath. "What did they say?"

He shrugs. "It doesn't matter."

Yeah, it does. But I know dealing with his family is a raw subject, so I don't press him further. The last thing I want to do is cause him more stress. He's dealing with enough just being back in Paradise.

"What are your plans today?" I pick up the mug and sip the warm, smooth coffee. It has just a hint of vanilla. I look at Caleb over the rim and wish I didn't feel like the clock is ticking when it comes to the amount of time we can spend together. The more we're together, the more I want to be with him.

"I was wondering if you want to hang out," he says.

"Sure. What do you want to do? I know Lenny and Julio are staying with you, so I'm sure you can't ditch them all day."

"We're all going frolfing. You know, disc golf."

"Frolfing?" I've never been frolfing before. I'm not even sure I can play with my limp. "Why don't you and the guys go play, and we can meet up after."

Caleb shakes his head. "Mags, you're going. It's kind of a date thing. We're playing in pairs."

"A date thing?"

"Yeah. Get ready, 'cause we're meeting on the course at eleven."

"I've never played. We're going to lose."

"I figured as much."

I instinctively throw what I'm folding. Oops. A pair of panties, which he catches in one hand and holds up. It's a neutral-colored pair, without any designs.

"Please tell me these are your mom's."

"They're mine."

One of his eyebrows go up. "Maggie, panties are supposed to be sexy. These aren't. I hope you have one of these in every color to bring to Spain."

I snatch them back and shove them to the bottom of the basket. "What's wrong with my underwear?"

"They're not sexy."

"They're comfy."

That makes Caleb laugh. "Just be ready at eleven. Enjoy the rest of the coffee before it gets cold."

An hour later, he's back to pick me up. He's got a bunch of discs in a backpack. I swallow my insecurity about playing because Caleb is so dead set on me joining them.

To my surprise, Trish and Leah are coming with us as well as Lenny and Julio. It's great to see Trish, but … are she and Lenny a couple? They're arguing about something, and Leah and Julio are walking ahead of us, obviously having a serious, private conversation.

I guess we're all a bunch of mismatched couples—that actually fit.

"Where's Erin?" I ask Trish.

"My mom was taking her to the doctor today for a sonogram," Trish explains. "Hopefully she's having a girl. Boys are gross." She gestures to Lenny. "My case in point."

"You haven't even seen me be gross, girl," Lenny says.

I don't want to, either.

"Explain how to play," I say to Lenny, diverting the argument. Lenny seems to be the frolfing expert in our group.

"It's simple. It's playing golf, but with discs instead of golf balls. Instead of eighteen holes of golf, there are eighteen metal baskets. The goal is to make the least amount of tries for each basket. Get it?"

"I think so."

Caleb takes my hand in his as we walk to the park. Not once do I feel like he's frustrated that I can't move faster. In fact, everyone slows their pace to match mine.

Only Leah seems uneasy. Every time she glances back

at me as I walk along, she quickly looks away. She knows I'm aware she was the one who hit me, but we don't talk about it. I know talking about it will bring out raw emotions for both of us, so I avoid the subject.

Am I mad that Leah ran into me? Yes, but I can't change it, and I know she didn't do it on purpose. It took me a long time to come to terms with what happened to me. It used to eat at me every single day. I was mad and upset and felt so sorry for myself I pretty much stopped remembering what life was all about.

Then Caleb got out of jail, and I learned that life was worth living. He made me realize I should stop living in the past and enjoy the present, no matter what. For example, I can still play tennis, the sport I've always loved with a passion—I just have to play differently now. I can't run, but I can still hit the ball with the racquet.

I've come to terms with the accident and the result of it. The biggest problem is that Leah still struggles with her role in what happened that night.

I do wish she'd come clean and tell the world that she was the one who hit me, but doing that has major consequences. I'm not sure she's ready for those consequences. She may never be.

At the frolf course, Caleb hands me three discs. "One is for long range, one is for mid range, and this is a putter disc—only use it when you're close to the basket."

"Got it."

"Just so you know, Lenny, this isn't a date," Trish says.

"Then what is it?"

"It's me feeling sorry for you, because you're such a loser."

Lenny tosses his disc up in the air and catches it. "Okay, Trish, so if I'm such a loser you won't mind making a bet with me. If I beat you, you agree this is a date and you have to promise to scream at the top of your lungs that I'm a fucking stud and you've had a crush on me since you met me."

"And what if I beat you?" Trish asks, rubbing her hands together. There's fire in her eyes.

"Name your price."

I wince. I'm afraid of Lenny and Trish challenging each other, because whenever they're involved there is sure to be drama and craziness.

"If I win," Trish says, "you have to come to my house and clean my room ... and all of our toilets. For a week." She crosses her arms on her chest, looking pretty pleased with herself.

"Fine," Lenny says.

"Fine," Trish says. "Let's shake on it."

"Oh, no. We're gonna kiss on it."

He puts his arm around her waist and pulls her forward. I thought for sure Trish would slap him or knee him in the groin, but she doesn't. She kisses him back. I turn away, because it's sloppy and they make noises that should only be made in private.

"Ugh, I just lost my appetite," Julio chimes in as he

watches Trish and Lenny go at it. "Break it up before Leah and I ditch you guys and go somewhere else."

As he says that, Kendra comes walking up to the frolf course.

"Hey," she says. "Sorry I'm late."

I step away from Caleb. "Did you invite her?"

"Yeah," he says. "I did."

THIRTY-THREE

Caleb

Maggie's shoulders are slumped. She stopped smiling as soon as Kendra showed up. I know things are tense with Kendra and Maggie right now, but as long as I'm in Paradise, I can't ignore Brian. And where Brian is, Kendra is.

I just didn't expect Kendra to come alone.

"Where's Brian?" I ask her.

"We broke up last night. The wedding is off."

"The hell it is," Brian says, appearing off in the distance. He's walking in a crooked line, as if he's on something.

"Go away," Kendra tells him.

"No," Brian slurs. He reaches for her. "You're my partner."

Kendra pushes Brian out of arms reach. "Not anymore."

"Can we start the game already and stop bickering, everyone?" Julio says.

When Julio talks, people listen. Even Kendra and Brian, who ignore each other even though they're partners in this game.

We start tossing our discs toward the baskets. At first Maggie is horrible. Her disc flies about ten feet in front of her, and she's not even using the putter disc.

"Flick your wrist," I tell her.

She tries, but the disc flies backwards and almost hits Kendra in the head.

Maggie's hand flies over her mouth as the disc whizzes past Kendra. "Oops, sorry."

"I bet," Kendra mutters.

Brian tells Kendra to be nice. She sneers at him and I think *oh, buddy, you are going to pay for that remark later.*

Moving from one fairway to another isn't easy for Maggie, who has to tread lightly on the uneven ground. At one point when she stumbles and falls, I almost offer to take her home.

"Hop on my back," I tell her instead, as we head to the next fairway.

She looks at me as if I'm crazy.

"Come on, Mags. It'll be fun."

"No, it won't," she says. When I take her discs and bend down so she can easily maneuver onto my back, she asks, "You sure about this?"

Yeah, I'm sure. "Just hop on." She grabs my shoulders

and I carry her to the next hole. "You suck at this game. The last one was a par three, and how you managed to get an eight on it is embarrassing. I think I need to give you private lessons, so next time we can kick a little frolf ass."

"Private lessons sound good," she says, then kisses the back of my neck.

"You guys are dorks," Kendra says when we finally arrive at the next hole. I kneel so Maggie can slide off my back without too much stress on her leg.

"Don't call my best friend a dork, Kendra," Brian says.

Kendra puts her hand on her hip and flips her hair back. Oh, no. That's not a good sign. "Don't defend him. And he's not just your friend, Brian. He's my ex."

"He was my best friend before either of us dated you."

"We slept together behind his back," Kendra spits back with venom. "Some best friend you turned out to be."

With those words, Brian takes something out of the waistband of his jeans. It's a flask.

"Man, what're you doing?" I ask.

"None of your business."

Oh, shit. This is not happening. Not in front of Lenny and Julio and my sister. And not in front of Maggie, who hates Kendra drama more than anything. I want her to forget my past, not be reminded of it.

Kendra tosses one of the discs, aiming directly at Brian's nuts. Brian barely dodges the disc, takes another swig of whatever he's got in the flask, and looks his fiancé right in the eye. "Let's have a contest."

Lenny's eyes light up. The dude loves challenges more than anything.

Julio leans into me and says so nobody else can hear, "*These* are your friends? They're all fuckin' lunatics."

And this is coming from a guy who's been in jail for robbery and money laundering.

"Tell you what," Brian says, getting really pissed at Kendra now. I can tell because his face is getting all red and splotchy. That only happens right after he works out or when he's really pissed. "If I win the next hole, the wedding's back on. If you win, you're free to call it off and be with Caleb."

Um, not happening. "Brian, don't be an idiot," I tell him, but he's not listening. I don't know if he's high on top of being drunk. He's definitely not himself.

"Agreed," Kendra says, ignoring me. "But it's not a fair matchup."

"Fine. You pick who throws for me, and I pick who throws for you."

Maggie attempts to hide behind me.

"I pick Maggie. She'll throw for you," Kendra says through clenched teeth.

"Then *I* pick Leah," Brian says.

"Can I opt out?" Maggie asks them.

A red-faced Brian and a raging Kendra both say "no" at the same time.

"Guys, just kiss and make up already," I tell them. "You're pregnant, Kendra. And it's not happening between us, so get over it."

"Shut up, Caleb," Kendra says, venom in her voice.

"I got this," Maggie says, a fierce and determined look on her face.

I get it.

Maggie's fighting for me. She wants to win me, fair and square. Doesn't she realize she already has me, and doesn't have to fight?

I watch in awe as my girl takes a disc in her hand and goes to the tee.

"Maggie…" I say. "Umm…You grabbed a putter. That won't go too far."

I hold out another disc for her, which she takes with a murmured thanks.

Maggie takes a deep breath, then lets it rip with an impressive grunt. She winces when it veers to the right and almost lands in some bushes.

Her hand flies to her mouth in horror.

"Good goin', babe," I joke.

"It's not funny," she says, taking this competition way too seriously.

My sister is next. Julio tries to give her some pointers, but I'm not sure my twin sis wants Kendra to win. My sister whips the disc, but it also veers and lands in the bushes.

Oh, man, this is torture.

In the end, it's neck and neck. My sister holds her putter while Maggie holds hers.

"Wait," Maggie says before Leah aims for the metal basket.

Leah stills.

Maggie holds her disc at her side. "I can't do this."

"Me neither," Leah adds.

Maggie limps up to Kendra. "I don't play games with people's lives like you do."

'Atta girl!

Maggie drops the disc at Kendra's feet. "If you let him go and he doesn't come back to you, he wasn't yours to begin with. It's a lesson I learned in first grade."

Man, my girl is one tough chick when she wants to be. I wonder if it has something to do with those big, comfy granny panties she's got on.

Maggie limps away, my sister at her side. It reminds me of when we were kids and they were inseparable. I like that they're figuring out how to be friends again.

I watch until Maggie and Leah are out of sight.

"I'm out of here," Kendra says, storming off to her car.

"Me too," Brian says, turning to storm off to his.

I step in front of him. "I can't let you do that."

"Why not?"

"Because you're drunk. I can't let you drive while you're fucked up."

"Move out of my way, Caleb, and don't be such a dork."

"I'm a dork, too," Lenny says. "'Cause I won't let you drive, either."

"Give Caleb your keys," Trish orders Brian. "Now!"

Damon the Enforcer would be proud of us Re-START misfits. Too bad he's not here to see us all in action.

THIRTY-FOUR
Maggie

I head toward home with Leah.

"Thanks for that," Leah says. "I was gonna miss on purpose. I never liked Kendra."

I stop and turn to her. "What would you think about Caleb and me as a couple?"

She doesn't answer. Her non-answer is my answer.

"I'm leaving for Spain in less than two weeks, so you won't have to see us together for much longer." My words come out quick and I know she can tell I'm upset. "Leah, something's gotta give."

I limp away from her now, but I hear Caleb calling after me.

"Where's everyone else?" I ask.

"Lenny ended up driving Brian home—he was pretty wasted—and Julio and Trish went with them," Caleb says. "Listen Maggie. About the game . . . I'm sorry." He moves in front of me. "I shouldn't have forced that situation on you. I just thought we could be a normal couple and—"

"We'll never be a normal couple, Caleb. We have so much baggage it's ridiculous." I hold a hand up when I see he's about to protest. "I'm living in reality. Reality is that Kendra still wants you in her life and your sister still wants me out of your life—it's easier on her that way."

Just thinking about Kendra and Leah is overwhelming right now. "I need to get away from here," I tell him.

"Where are you going?"

I take out the keys to my car. "Where I always go to think."

"If it's any consolation," he says, "I don't give a shit what anyone else thinks about us being together."

"I know. I wish I didn't care, but I do."

When I get to my car, I immediately head over to Mrs. Reynolds' house. Lou isn't there, and neither is the *For Sale* sign. A sinking feeling forms the pit of my stomach when I think about someone else living in this house.

As I finger the white-painted wood of the gazebo, I think about what I said to Caleb. I know he's still struggling being at home where he doesn't feel like he belongs. I saw where he's been sleeping—on the couch in his living room.

Lenny can't stay in the Beckers' house forever. I don't

know why he doesn't have a home or family to go back to after our Re-START trip, but he's obviously sleeping at the Beckers' because he has nowhere else to go.

And Julio was practically begging for a place to stay.

Even though I don't want to, I need to brace myself for the inevitable. Caleb is in my life temporarily. When I leave for Spain, we'll be going our separate ways. Should I make the most out of what we have now? Reality is, Caleb will soon be out of my life for good.

THIRTY-FIVE

Caleb

Two days after the frolf game, I'm standing in front of my sister's bedroom door. Lenny and Julio went out, and my dad is at work. It's the perfect time to have it out with Leah.

I knock on the door and wait. She cracks it, but doesn't let me in.

"Do you need something?"

"Yeah," I say. "We need to talk."

She opens her door wide and sits on the edge of her bed. Her room used to have posters of guys in boy bands, but now she's got pictures of skulls and crossbones and posters that remind me of death.

It's too fucked up for words.

"You've got to come clean to Mom and Dad." There, I said it. "I'm done taking the fall. It wasn't just telling the cops I was the one driving. It wasn't just pleading guilty and being locked up in jail for almost a year. Our lie is like a fucking cancer that's spread to every single area of our lives." I point to the posters on her wall. "You do realize this is your cry for help. It's sick shit, Leah."

The more I look at those skull pictures staring at me with their empty-holed eyes, the more I want to rebel against it. I'm not dead. I don't want to be dead. I don't want my sister to be dead. And I sure as hell don't want to be haunted by the past anymore.

"You promised," she says in an eerily calm voice. "When I told you about the accident, you said you'd take care of it."

"I was *drunk*, Leah. I hardly knew what I was doing, and by the time I realized I shouldn't have lied to the police, it was too late."

"I was scared."

"And I wasn't?" I snap. But maybe she didn't know how I was feeling, because I masked every emotion I had after I got arrested. I take a deep breath and try again. "It's time to tell Mom and Dad."

I look up and see a picture of a skeleton with its teeth sunk into a heart and I can't take it anymore . . . I rake my fingers across the wall and rip them all down. "I'm done with you looking like death warmed over. I hate what you did to Maggie. I hate it, and I hate you for making me promise to take our secret to the grave and then paying me back by being a fucking recluse."

"Caleb, lay off her."

I turn to see Julio standing in the doorway.

"Stay out of this, Julio," I growl.

Instead of listening to me, Julio walks into the room and stands next to my sister. "I said *lay off*."

Is he kidding me? "This doesn't have anything to do with you."

"Yes, it does," Leah murmurs. She looks up at me with tear-filled eyes. "Because last night Julio and I stayed up all night and talked. He convinced me to turn myself in."

Huh?

I didn't expect that. I expected a lot of things to come out of my sister's mouth, but not that.

Relief floods all my senses, followed by worry and fear. What will happen when she turns herself in? Will she have to serve time? Those questions have been running through my head every time I thought about what would happen if Leah confessed.

How was it Julio who convinced her to come clean?

"Leah's tougher than she thinks," Julio says as he puts his arm around her shoulder. "She can do this." He squeezes her shoulders and looks into her eyes. "You can do this."

"You've known my sister all of three days, Julio."

"Yeah, and I bet I know her better than you."

Just when I'm about to laugh at that ridiculous com-ment, Leah says, "Julio's right. For the longest time I wanted to tell you how I felt, but I couldn't. You were sad or angry or pissed off…and I was afraid of hurting you again."

My sister chokes back tears and runs into my arms. "I'm so sorry about what I did to you. Julio told me how it was in jail for the two of you, and I'm just...so sorry." She swipes at her eyes and says, "I think we need to call Dad and have him meet us at the rehab center. Whether Mom realizes it or not, she needs her son back."

An hour later I'm sitting in the waiting room of New Horizons Recovery Center. My dad didn't really want us to have this meeting because he thinks my mom's emotional status is too fragile, but when Leah and I said we were coming to see her with or without him, he agreed to meet us.

A woman with the name *Rachel* on her nametag greets us, then has us go into what's called a group therapy room to wait for my mom. It makes me feel stiff and uncomfortable, because we had mandatory group therapy sessions when I was in jail. I have to remind myself that this isn't jail. My mom wants to be here. She could leave on her own, but has chosen to stay because she doesn't trust herself not to use prescription drugs as a crutch when things get tough.

"You can have a seat, Caleb," Rachel says in a soft voice probably meant to calm me.

I try not to pace back and forth in the room like a caged animal, but I can't sit because I've got a bunch of pent-up nervous energy. "No, thanks."

The chairs are situated in a circle. My dad is sitting in one chair in his three-piece suit and tie. My sister, surprisingly, isn't slumped in her chair. She's sitting straight up and has a determined look on her face. If Julio was the one who talked her into facing all this crap head-on, he's a fucking genius.

My sister doesn't know it yet, but I'm not abandoning her. She's not the only one who made mistakes the night of the accident.

As soon as my mom walks in the room in grey sweats with the New Horizons logo on the front, I realize she's different. Her face is drawn and her spirit seems somehow … lost.

My first instinct is to go up and hug her but I figure out, by the way she has her hands folded on her chest, that she doesn't want any affection from me or anyone else in the room.

Mom stops in her tracks when she sees me step toward her. "Why are you here?"

My veins are pumping hard and I'm so damn tense my arms are stiff at my sides. This is already a billion times harder than I imagined. "I came back. Maggie told me you guys needed me. At first I didn't want to believe her …"

"You left me. A good son doesn't leave his mother."

Her words cut deep. Oh, man, I should never have left. I thought it would be best, that everything would be okay if the "Caleb Quotient" was out of the equation. I was wrong. I've managed to screw up so much in such a short amount of time.

"I'm sorry, Mom."

Deflated, I sit in the chair next to Leah.

"I'm sorry, too," Leah says. "I need to apologize to everyone in this family."

My sister turns to me and puts her hand on my knee. I put my hand on top of hers.

I feel her hesitation and fear as if it's my own. But I also feel her determination to set the wrongs of the past right.

"Mom, Dad," Leah says after I nod to her, giving her silent support. "I was the one who hit Maggie the night of the accident."

Watching the expression change on my parents' faces is pure torture. At first they cock their heads to the side as if they've heard the words wrong. When Leah doesn't say anything else, the reality of what she said starts to sink in.

"No," my mom whispers, shaking her head. "No. No."

"What are you saying, Leah?" my dad asks, his voice about to crack. "*What. Are. You. Saying?*"

A stream of tears start flowing down Leah's face. "I was at the party. I'd had maybe two beers. When I was driving home, I swerved to hit a squirrel. I didn't mean to hit Maggie." She's choking on her tears now, and I look up at the ceiling in an attempt to hold myself in check.

It's not working.

Dammit.

Tears start forming in my eyes. I try to blink them back, but it's no use. Seeing my sister so upset, seeing my dad and mom frozen in shock, and knowing that one fateful night destroyed my family and permanently damaged Maggie's leg is just too much for me.

I dab at my own tears and attempt an explanation.

"When Leah came back to the party all freaked out, I told her I'd take care of it," I tell them. "I was so wasted that night, I wasn't thinking straight. When the cops asked who was driving, I said it was me."

"Oh, God, Caleb, I'm so sorry," Leah cries out. "I don't know how you could ever forgive me. I don't deserve forgiveness for the hell I put you through."

She buries her head in her hands.

"I can't believe this is happening," my dad says. "This *can't* be happening."

"No," my mom says again.

I look over at Rachel. I think she was expecting a regular family therapy session, and from her deer-in-headlights look I think we've shocked her into silence.

I nod. "It's true." Man, I feel a sort of freedom I haven't felt in a long time. I want to share this with Maggie. I guess now is as good a time as any to say the other piece of news I've been holding back.

"I know this is another bomb I'm dropping, but Maggie Armstrong and I are dating. I didn't mean for it to happen. I denied it for a long time, then hid it for a while ... and I'm not gonna do that anymore."

"Does she know ..." my dad says, his voice trailing off. I know he's on the brink of breaking down. I can see it in his trembling lip and shaking hands.

"Yeah, she knows." I look over at Leah. "Maggie knows everything."

My mom looks at me. It's the first time she's looked at me without contempt or scorn since I was arrested. She keeps shaking her head, as if she's trying to wrap her brain around this new, totally unexpected information. "Leah, how could you?" Mom asks, her words coming out slow. "How could you stand by and let your brother go to jail for something you did?"

"I don't know, Mom. I don't know. But I'm going to make it right." Her puffy, bloodshot eyes meet mine. "I'm turning myself in tomorrow."

THIRTY-SIX

Maggie

"Maggie, can I come over?" Caleb's voice comes through the phone. He doesn't sound happy.

"Sure. What's wrong?"

"I'll tell you when I get there."

My mom and Lou are right downstairs. I haven't told her about Caleb. I wanted to. To be honest, I've been stalling because the last thing I want to do is upset her when she's still trying to figure things out with my dad and Lou.

It's time I confess to my mom the truth about me and Caleb.

Lou and my mom are in the kitchen. They're both chopping vegetables for some sort of soup concoction they're making. She's still not wearing his ring, but he's come over every day and is really fighting for the right to be with her forever. She made my dad postpone his move here … indefinitely.

"Mom, can I talk to you?"

My mom, complete with flour in her hair and a carrot in her hand, looks up from the cutting board. "Is anything wrong?"

"No. It's just that … if it weren't for Caleb, I might have given up on life."

My mom stops chopping. "What?"

"After the accident, it was Caleb who made me realize life was worth living."

"Maggie, that's a bunch of nonsense."

"No, Mom, it's not. You want to know why?"

"I'm sure you're going to tell me no matter what I say."

I don't know how she's going to react. She's not exactly happy, but at least she's listening. "Because he pulled me out of my depression. You didn't even see it because you were so happy I was home and not living in hospitals anymore. But I wasn't happy. I was miserable until Caleb came back from jail and helped me realize I was worth something even though I had a disability."

"Why are you telling me this now?" my mom asks.

"Because he's coming over, and I want you to be prepared …" The doorbell rings. "That's him, Mom. Just, be nice and don't judge him until I tell you everything."

I rush to open the door. Caleb's bloodshot eyes greet me. He doesn't say anything; he just pulls me close and hugs me tight right on the front steps of my house.

"I saw my mom today," he mumbles into my hair. "Oh, God, Maggie, it was so awful. Leah told our parents she was the one who hit you."

I know that was probably the hardest thing Leah has ever done. "How is she?"

"She was crying. A lot." He pulls away, but holds on to my hands. "She's determined to turn herself in. I don't know what's going to happen. I just called Damon. He's coming over tomorrow to advise us on what to do."

I touch Caleb's forehead to mine. I can see in his face how much this is tearing him apart. "I'm sorry. I'll go with you. Whatever I can do to help, I will."

"What's going on?" my mom asks, confused. "I don't know why you're here," she says to Caleb. "And pray tell, why are you two holding hands?"

I take a deep breath and squeeze Caleb's hand. We're going to do this together. I lead him inside my house and stand before my mom and Lou. "Caleb and I have something to tell you both." I look at Caleb through watery eyes. "I know this is going to be a shock, but try and understand..."

This has got to be one of the toughest days of Caleb's life. While he's freeing himself from blame, the reality is that he's incriminating his sister at the same time. "I wasn't the one who hit Maggie," he says. He clears his throat. "Umm..." He holds my hand tight. "It was Leah."

"You're lying."

"He's not, Mom," I tell her.

"Why?" my mom asks, tears now streaming down her face. I'm crying, too.

Caleb gives a half-shrug. "I thought I could handle it better than Leah. I thought I was sparing her from going through something that would ruin her. I could handle going to jail, but my sister couldn't. The whole thing just kind of spiraled out of control, and I realized I was wrong, but it was too late." He looks at me. "And Maggie was caught in the middle of it all."

Lou walks out of the room for a minute, then reappears with a box of tissues. He hands a few to my mom. She dabs her eyes with the tissue. "This is a lot to take in. Maggie, did you know about this?"

I nod.

"How could you not say anything? I'm your mother."

"I didn't figure it out until right before Caleb left. I didn't say anything because I wanted Caleb to be the one to reveal it. Somehow I felt it was his secret to tell. Besides, I was desperate to stop reliving the accident. I wanted it over. I needed to move on for my own sanity." I look up at the boy who filled the void in my life. "Caleb helped me realize I couldn't stop living my life because of my disability."

My mom shakes her head. "I need time to digest this. This is just … too much for me. I need to be alone right now."

She hurries up the stairs. A minute later, I hear her door shut, and I wince. I never wanted to hurt her or make her feel betrayed by either of us.

The Re-START program really brought home the fact that accidents affect so many people … they're like avalanches, affecting everyone and everything in their wake.

I look over at Lou. "I'm sorry. I didn't mean to upset her."

"I know. I think it'll take a while to sink in. Give her some time and she'll come around." Lou turns to Caleb. "You were brave to come back here."

"I don't feel brave right now. My home life is kind of a mess, and I have two guys staying at my parents' with me 'cause they're dealing with the same kind of fallout I'm dealing with."

Lou pauses for a moment, then smiles. "I have a proposition for you," he says to Caleb. "My mother's house is vacant. If you and your friends want to stay there for a while, and pay enough rent to cover the utilities and taxes on the property, it's yours."

"Are you serious, sir?" Caleb asks, totally shocked.

Lou nods. "I know my mother thought you were a good kid and wanted to help you. I figure this is fate; it's the way my mom would want it. What do you say?"

Caleb shakes Lou's hand vigorously. "I'd say you've got yourself a deal."

When I'm walking with Caleb back to his house so we can spend time with Leah and give the good news to Lenny and Julio, Caleb says, "Lou's a good guy."

"I know. I hope my mom gets over her fear of loving someone other than my dad."

"What are your fears?" he asks. "About us, I mean."

"After today I have none, because"—I give him the honest answer, which I've held in for way too long—"because I love you."

THIRTY—SEVEN

Caleb

It felt incredible hearing Maggie tell me she loved me yesterday. But now I feel as helpless as the day Judge Farkus handed down his sentence to me. I'm sitting at the police station in a remote lobby with my sister, my dad, my mom, Maggie, Julio, and even Lenny, who said he wanted to come because he already feels like part of our family. (Of course that was before he met my mom, who told him to sit straight and cut his hair or he wouldn't be invited to Thanksgiving dinner, which is over three months away.)

My cousin Heath is a lawyer, and he's here too. He'll be in the room with Leah when she confesses to hitting Maggie.

"You ready, Leah?" Damon asks as he kneels in front of my sister. He came to our house this morning and very calmly explained that the easiest way would be to make a sworn statement at the police station. Then Leah will be processed into the system. Damon stressed that it's all up to the state prosecutor to decide whether or not to go ahead and formally charge Leah, since the accident is still within the three-year statute of limitations. My record will be wiped clean, regardless.

My knee is shaking.

I look over at Maggie, who looks equally nervous. She didn't have to come, but she did. Hell, if I were her I'd probably be demanding that Leah be locked up for at least as long as I was, if not more.

But Maggie's not me. She's got a good, forgiving spirit. Just being around her makes me strive to be a better person.

Damon told my parents and me to write letters in support of Leah, vouching for her character. He said he'll attach it to the confession, so the state prosecutor or the judge assigned to the case will take it into consideration when deciding her sentence.

"I'm ready," Leah says with a weak smile. This can't be easy for her, that's for sure. But she's stronger than I ever gave her credit for. This morning when she walked down the stairs, she didn't have anything black on. She's wearing white pants and a yellow shirt. She looks so different, so ... bright.

"Good morning, sunshine," my dad had said after taking one look at her.

I thought we'd all be somber and crying, but we've held it together so far. When my mom called last night and said she wanted to leave rehab and come with us to the police station, I felt like the Beckers were starting to heal.

We just have to get over this one last hurdle.

Heath and Damon gesture to my sister to follow them.

"Wait," Damon says, stopping. "Do you have those letters I can attach to her statement?"

After we hand them over, Maggie pulls a piece of paper out of her purse and hands it to him. "Leah, I know you're not doing this for me, but ... thanks."

It's a hugfest now, all of us hoping to transfer our strength to Leah before her confession. Even Lenny gets up to hug my sister, then turns and hugs me.

"I owed you one," he says to me. "I owe you more than one, actually. You gave me a family, something I haven't had in a long time."

I nod. Believe it or not, Lenny's grown on me.

Leah is still hugging Maggie. "I never meant to hurt you, you know that, right?"

"You've apologized about a million times," Maggie says, with tears in her eyes. "You *never* have to say it again, okay? I forgive you. It happened, it was a mistake."

They hug again, and then my sister heads for the heavy metal door. On the other side of that door she'll confess. Then she'll be booked, complete with fingerprints and a mug shot.

"Hey, Leah," Julio barks out.

Leah turns around.

"Remember what I said," he says, then winks at her.

She holds her head up high and smiles at him. Then she nods to Heath and Damon. "Let's do this."

When she's gone, it's eerily quiet. Until Lenny turns to my dad and says, "Pull my finger."

THIRTY-EIGHT

Maggie

Five exhausting hours later we're back at home. They released Leah on a five thousand dollar bond, so we're all together. I was so worried about Leah today, but she seemed okay about everything. She actually said finally telling the truth made her feel free, which is weird because she might have to serve jail time. Damon said he was going to talk to the prosecutor, and try to convince him not to charge Leah.

Caleb's mom decided to come back home, so everyone is happy but definitely on edge.

Caleb, Lenny, and Julio are moving into Mrs. Reynolds' house at the end of the week. Caleb and the guys are going to work for Caleb's uncle, who owns a construction company. He said he'll get his GED and get his life back on track.

The night before I leave for Spain, Caleb and I walk to the park and stand under the big oak tree. Our time together is ticking down by the minute, and I'm nervous.

"I wish you could come with me."

He gives a short laugh. "Me too."

"Before you leave, I gotta get something off my chest." He steps back, brushes a hand through his hair, and starts pacing. "Listen, I'm really fucking scared about you leaving. I'm sorry for cussing, but it's true. While I know I can go on without you, dammit, I don't want to. I've gotten used to having you in my life, and it just won't be the same without you."

My heart is beating fast and I reach out to hold his hand. "What are you saying?"

"I'm saying that I love you, Maggie." He looks at me through crystal clear eyes. "I was holding back and didn't want to say it, because I didn't want you to think I said it as some ploy to make you not date other guys while you're in Spain."

"I don't want to date other guys."

"That's what they all say, until some good-looking Spanish dude comes up to you and whispers some romantic Spanish shit in your ear and asks you out."

I laugh. "I don't see that happening."

"What if it does? What if you meet some guy and decide to stay in Spain forever?"

"I can say the same thing, Caleb. Not the staying in Spain thing, but what if you meet some girl while I'm gone?"

"Not gonna happen," he says, repeating my words.

I know he doesn't want to force me to make a commitment to him. The truth is, I want him to be free this next year. If we can make it through this, I know we'll be strong enough to last forever if we want. "I propose this," I say. "We promise not to go looking for someone else, but if it happens it happens and we have to be honest with each other about it."

"Deal. Now let's stop talking about it before I decide to convince you to stay in Paradise."

"What do you want to do?" I ask. "Kiss?"

"Oh, yeah. I want to kiss."

He pulls me toward him and I feel his warm body against mine. Caleb makes me feel happy and protected and loved all at the same time. He kisses me, his full soft lips making my body shudder with excitement. I can't imagine anything feeling this good. "This is perfect," I tell him.

He gently swipes his lips across mine. "It's pretty damn close."

Nine Months Later

"Welcome to Chicago's O'Hare International Airport. Please wait until the aircraft has come to a complete stop before deplaning."

My heart is beating so furiously in my chest I'm surprised the other passengers can't hear it. I gather my backpack when the plane stops and quickly limp toward the baggage claim, ignoring the pain in my stiff leg.

Caleb's not here. My mom is, though. She rushes up to me and hugs me tight. Lou is with her, so I hope that's a good sign. She's not wearing his ring, but the last time I talked to her she asked me what I thought of winter weddings. My dad visited me in Spain for New Year's, and we hashed out a lot of issues. I think we're on the mend, and even though he'll never be a doting father, I'm glad we've started to work things out.

"Did you have a nice flight?" Lou asks. "I bet you're hungry for some good ol' American food."

"I'm definitely hungry for one of Irina's pies from the diner," I tell him, and get a smile in response. Everyone loves Irina's pies, and I've been her taste tester ever since my mom started working there.

When we have my luggage and are driving back to Paradise, my mom drills me on how my leg is holding up. I answer her, but the entire time all I can think is, *where is Caleb?*

The last email I got from him said he'd meet me right when I got home. That was almost three weeks ago, though. A lot could have changed in three weeks.

I tell myself I'm over-thinking things. Ugh, I can't take the suspense.

"Have you heard from Caleb?" I ask, trying not to sound like I'm desperate to hear the answer.

"He came by this afternoon and left you a note in your room," my mom says.

A note. Notes are bad. Notes can't be good.

"Did he say anything when he left the note?"

My mom shakes her head. "No. He just asked if he could leave a note and I said it was okay. He was in the house less than two minutes."

I wish the ride home didn't take over an hour. The entire plane ride, I'd imagined hundreds of different scenarios of our reunion. None of them included a note.

At my house, I get out of the car and head inside after Lou insists on bringing my luggage up.

Upstairs, my bedroom is the same as I left it. My bed is made and on top of my big comforter is an envelope. On the front, one word is written in Caleb's handwriting: *Maggie.*

I pick up the envelope with trembling fingers and rip open the seal. I unfold the note slowly. I close my eyes and take a deep breath, then I open them and read what it says:

Do you remember the old oak tree? Go there, and wait for me.

Huh? The old oak at Paradise Park?

I tell my mom I'll be back later. She doesn't argue, probably because I'm practically out the door before I even finish my sentence.

It's dusk now, but the park isn't far away. I head for the oak tree. Nobody is here, except for a little squirrel running across the grass.

I wait ten minutes, staring up at the tree and wondering why he wanted me to wait here and how long he wants me to wait. Just as I'm starting to feel insecure, I see a silhouette running toward me.

I'd recognize Caleb anywhere. My heart soars.

"Maggie!"

He stands in front of me, toe-to-toe, totally out of breath. He's wearing ripped jeans and a stained white T-shirt. He looks like he hasn't shaved in a week, and his hair is disheveled.

"I'm so sorry I'm late." He reaches out and fingers my hair, which is long now since I haven't cut it in almost a year. "You look great, Maggie. Different."

"Thanks," I say. "You do, too."

I reach up and put my arms around his neck, not caring that I'm being bold. I don't want to hold back. "I missed you," I tell him.

His hands go around my waist and he pulls me close. "I have so many questions to ask you. But first..."

I think we're going to kiss, but instead he pulls something out of his pocket and holds it up. It's a bandanna.

"What's that for?" I ask.

"Turn around."

I cock an eyebrow.

"Trust me, Maggie."

I do as he says. "I was going to kiss you," I tell him.

He gently positions the bandanna over my eyes and ties it in the back. "You will. I promise. Just...be patient."

I'm not patient.

While I was in Spain, my feelings for Caleb grew infinitely stronger. I had guy friends my roommate and I would go out with, but none of them made me shiver with excitement. I get excited just thinking about being in Caleb's arms again.

"I can't see anything," I announce as I'm led across the park and into a car.

"That's pretty much the point, sweetheart."

I feel us winding through streets until we come to a

stop. He opens the door and leads me out of the car. He chuckles as he puts his hands on my waist and urges me forward to who knows where.

"Where are we?" I ask, wondering how long it will be before the suspense is over.

"You'll know soon enough. Okay, stop."

"Can I take the blindfold off?"

"Nope. Not yet." In one swift movement, Caleb picks me up and cradles me in his arms.

I wrap my arms around his neck for support. "The last time you held me like this you dunked me in water."

He walks forward. "Trust me, Maggie."

"I do. But I've got to be honest and say you smell like a sweaty guy from the gym."

"I've been working. I promise to take a shower after I show you something.

He walks a little more, then suddenly stops. "Okay, pull off the blindfold."

When I do, I realize where we are immediately. In Mrs. Reynolds' gazebo. The entire floor is covered in cushions and little twinkling lights outline the perimeter. On top of the cushions are thousands of little white and red rose petals.

"It's perfect," I say breathlessly as I slide my sandals off and walk onto the cushions. "Where are Lenny and Julio?" I ask. I know Lou took the house off the market and pretty much considers it a haven for Caleb and his friends. As long as they're employed and don't get in trouble, they've got a roof over their head.

"I told them to sleep out tonight. Tonight I wanted to be alone with you."

I swallow, hard. "Alone?" Racy thoughts a girl shouldn't have clutter my mind. I smile. "Really?"

"Yeah. It's been so damn long I was afraid you were gonna return to Paradise and tell me you never wanted to see me again."

"I was afraid of the same thing about you," I admit.

We both laugh, and for some reason it makes me feel better that we're both cautious and nervous.

"Have you seen Kendra and Brian's new baby recently?" I ask. He told me he's been going out with Brian and his high school buddies on occasion.

"Yeah. Cute kid, although I've got a feeling Kendra's gonna raise her as a little diva."

"How's their relationship?" I ask.

"Rocky, but they're trying. Last time I saw Kendra, she hardly spoke to me. I suspect she realizes I'm not looking at her like she's the goddess she wants everyone to think she is."

"Good."

"Maggie, I want to tell you something," he says in a serious tone, as we settle down into the plush cushions.

I shake my head. "No. Let me say what I have to say first." This is not going to be easy. I take a deep breath, gathering the courage to put everything on the line. There are things that I've held back because I was scared, but I learned something in Spain this year. One of my professors said if you tiptoe into cold water, you're missing out on the rush of plunging in headfirst.

I'm going to plunge in, without worrying about the consequences. I look at Caleb, at the twinkling lights, and at the beautiful petals surrounding us.

"I've been holding back because I've been scared. You can crush my heart like my dad did with my mom. You have power over me." A tear escapes my eye. "I still love you, Caleb. I fell in love with you right here in this back-yard, and I never stopped. Being apart this year hasn't changed anything."

Caleb looks around, as if he's thinking of something to say but doesn't know how to put it into words. "Ever since we got locked in Mrs. Reynolds' attic, I knew I'd been missing out on a girl who really cared about me and wasn't self-absorbed. I was so blind for so long."

"What happens when I leave for college in the fall?"

"I'll come visit you whenever I can. U of I isn't far away." He touches my nose. "I want to kiss you, but I need to take a quick shower first." Hopping up off the cush-ions, Caleb starts walking toward the house. "Just...wait here and don't move until I get back. I have a surprise for you," he says with a nervous edge to his voice.

I'm confused, but I promise not to move until he comes back. I lean back on the cushions. It's just right, being back in Paradise with Caleb again. I know he's working construc-tion and trying to save up for college. He can do it. I'm sure of it.

He comes back ten minutes later, all cleaned up. His shirt outlines his arm muscles, which are bigger since the last time I saw him. I'm sure it's from working construction all day.

He looks at me with an intense expression. In the past, every time I caught him looking at me like that, I wanted to pinch myself. I thought the only way Caleb Becker would ever look at me like that was if I was dreaming or if he had an agenda.

I don't know when the switch happened. I think it was after Kendra stayed late at his house, talking. Afterward, he told me to trust him and asked me to be his girlfriend.

That was the moment.

The side of his mouth quirks up. "What're you thinking about?"

"You."

"I hope it's good."

I smile. "It is." I pat the cushions. We still haven't kissed, and I'm not interested in being patient right now. In fact, at this point I'd have no problem kissing a sweaty, rugged, smelly Caleb. "Come sit with me."

Instead of sitting with me, he holds out his hand. "I have a surprise for you."

He helps me up and hands me what looks like a remote control switch.

"You're not going to blindfold me again, are you?" I ask.

"No." He leads me behind the garage. I can barely see the outline of some kind of big structure. I can't make out what it is. Standing behind me, his arms holding me tight, Caleb whispers, "Push the button."

When I do, the entire structure lights up with twinkling lights … in the outline of … "A castle?"

A castle. A bigger version of that castle on the playground.

"I was finishing up the last-minute touches when your plane landed and lost track of time," Caleb says.

I can't believe I didn't notice it before. I don't know what to say … "It's a castle. I can't believe you made me a castle."

He takes my hand and leads me inside the structure. There are more petals strewn all over the wooden floor, surrounding a bunch of pillows and blankets in the middle.

"This is like heaven," I murmur as I look up into the open sky above us. It's just like it was at the park, but this is better. This time we aren't running away from anything or anyone.

Caleb sits down on the pillows. "Heaven, huh?"

"Definitely." I'm in shock as I sink down next to him. "This is amazing, Caleb. Did you build it yourself?"

"Lenny and Julio helped, but I designed it."

I look at the boy-turned-man who's the love of my life. I fish out a little box from my purse and hand it to him. "Here. It's a gift I brought back for you."

As he takes the top off and peers inside, I add, "I took a jewelry-making class." He pulls out the leather string and attached pendant. "It's a sword," I tell him.

He laughs. "I can tell what it is. It's really cool. I like it." He hangs it around his neck. I like that he's wearing something I made for him.

"It symbolizes strength," I say. "It reminds me of you."

In a surprise move, Caleb kneels in front of me. My heart just about leaps out of my chest.

He clears his throat.

He takes a deep breath and straightens his shoulders. "Okay, here's the deal. It was hell being apart from you this past year. Every day there was something that I did that reminded me of you."

I hold his face in my hands. When my lips are a whisper away from his, I ask, "Do you think we'll make it, Caleb? Do you think we'll last?"

"We've been to hell and back again. We're gonna make it. I love you, Maggie Armstrong, and always will."

"You promise?"

We lie back on the pillows together, and he places small, slow kisses across my neck. "Trust me," he whispers against my lips. "Maggie, you're my paradise."

About the Author

Simone was a teen in the '80s and still overuses words like "grody" and "totally," but she resists the urge to wear blue eye shadow or say "gag me with a spoon." When Simone's not writing, she's speaking to high schools or teaching writing. In her spare time, she watches reality television and teen movies. She lives near Chicago with her family and two dogs.

Simone loves to hear from her readers! Visit her at www.simoneelkeles.net.

See how Maggie and Caleb's story began in
Leaving paradise

Excerpt

ONE
Caleb

I've been waiting a year for this moment. It's not every day you get a chance to get out of jail. Sure, in the game of Monopoly you just have to roll the dice three times and wait for a double, or pay the fine and be free. But there are no games here at the Illinois Department of Corrections–Juvenile complex; or the DOC as we inmates call it.

Oh, it's not as rough as it sounds. The all male juvenile division is tough, but it's not like the adult DOC. You might ask why I've been locked up for the past year. I was convicted of hitting a girl with my car while driving drunk. It was a hit-and-run accident, too, which actually made the judge in my case royally pissed off. He tacked on an extra three months for that.

"You ready, Caleb?" Jerry, the cell guard, asks.

"Yes, sir." I've been waiting three hundred and ten days for this. Hell, yeah, I'm ready.

I take a deep breath and follow Jerry to the room where the review committee will evaluate me. I've been prepped by the other guys in my cell block. *Sit up straight, look full of remorse, act polite,* and all that stuff. But, to tell you the truth, how much can you trust guys who haven't gotten out themselves?

As Jerry opens the door to the evaluation room, my muscles start to twitch and I'm getting all sweaty beneath my state-issued coveralls, state-issued socks, and yep, even my state-issued briefs. Maybe I'm not so ready for this after all.

"Please sit down, Caleb," orders a woman wearing glasses and a stern look on her face.

I swear the scene is out of a bad movie. Seven people sitting behind six-foot-long tables in front of one lone metal chair.

I sit on the cold, hard metal.

"As you know, we're here to evaluate your ability to leave here and begin your life as a free citizen."

"Yes, ma'am," I say. "I'm ready to leave."

A big guy, who I can tell is going to play "bad cop," puts his hand up. "Whoa, slow down. We have a few questions to ask before we make our decision."

Oh, man. "Sorry."

Big Guy checks my file, flipping page after page. "Tell me about the night of the accident."

The one night in my life I want to erase from history. Taking a deep breath, I say, "I was drinking at a party. I drove home, but lost control of the car. When I realized I hit someone, I freaked and drove back to the party."

"You knew the girl you hit?"

Memories assault me. "Yes, sir. Maggie Armstrong... my neighbor." I don't add she was my twin sister's best friend.

"And you didn't get out of the car to see if your neighbor was hurt?"

I shift in my chair. "I guess I wasn't thinking straight."

"You *guess?*" another committee member asks.

"If I could turn back time, I swear I would. I'd change everything."

They question me for another half hour and I spurt out answers. Why I was drinking while underage, why I'd get into a car drunk, why I left the scene of the accident. I don't know if I'm saying the wrong thing or right thing, which puts me on edge. I'm just being me... seventeen-year-old Caleb Becker. If they believe me, I stand a chance of getting released early. If they don't... well, I'll be eating crappy food for another six months and continue rooming with convicts.

Big Guy looks right at me. "How do we know you won't go on another drinking binge?"

I sit up straight in my chair and direct my attention to each and every one of the committee members. "No offense, but I never want to come back here again. I made a huge mistake, one that's haunted me day and night since I've been here. Just...let me go home." For the first time in my life, I'm tempted to grovel.

Instead, I sit back and wait for another question.

"Caleb, please wait outside while we make our decision," the woman with the glasses says.

And it's over. Just like that.

I wait out in the hall. I'm usually not a guy who breaks under pressure, and the past year in jail has definitely given me an invisible piece of armor I wear around me. But waiting for a group of strangers to decide your fate is majorly nerve-wracking. I wipe beads of perspiration off my forehead.

"Don't worry," guard Jerry says. "If you didn't win them over, you might get another chance in a few months."

"Great," I mumble back, not consoled in the least.

Jerry chuckles, the shiny silver handcuffs hanging off his belt clinking with each movement. The dude likes his job too much.

We wait a half hour for someone to come out of the room and give me a sign of what's next. Freedom or more jail time?

I'm tired of being locked in my cell at night.

I'm tired of sleeping on a bunk bed with springs pushing into my back.

And I'm tired of being watched twenty-four hours a day by guards, personnel, cameras, and other inmates.

The lady with the glasses opens the door. "Caleb, we're ready for you."

She isn't smiling. Is that a bad sign? I'm bracing myself for bad news. I stand up and Jerry pats me on the back. A pity pat? Does he know something I don't? The suspense is freaking me out.

I sit back on the metal chair. All eyes are on me. Big Guy folds his hands on the table and says, "We all agree that your actions last year concerning the accident were reprehensible."

I know that. I *really* know that.

"But we believe that was an isolated incident never to be repeated. You've demonstrated positive leadership qualities with other inmates and worked hard on your jobs here. The review committee has decided to release you and have you finish out your sentence with one hundred and fifty hours of community service."

Does that mean what I think it means? "Release? As in I can leave here?" I ask the Big Guy.

"You'll be meeting with your transition coach tomorrow morning. He'll arrange your community service duties and report your progress to us."

Another member of the committee points a manicured finger at me. "If you screw up, your transition counselor can petition the judge to bring you back here to serve out the rest of your sentence. Do you understand?"

"Yes, sir."

"We don't give breaks to repeaters. Go back home, be a model citizen, finish your community service requirements, and have a good, clean life."

I *get it*. "I will," I say.

When I get back to my cell, the only one here is the new kid. He's twelve and still cries all the time. Maybe he should've thought twice before he buried a knife into the back of the girl who refused to go to the school dance with him.

"You ever gonna stop crying?" I ask the kid.

He's got his face in his pillow; I don't think he hears me. But then I hear a muffled, "I hate this place. I want to go home."

I change into my work boots because I get the pleasure of having to clean the dumpsters today. "Yeah, me too," I say. "But you're stuck here so you might as well suck it up and get with the program."

The kid sits up, sniffles, and wipes his nose with the back of his hand. "How long have you been here?"

"Almost a year."

That sets the kid plunging back into his pillow for more wailing. "I don't want to be locked up for a year," he cries.

Julio, another cell mate, walks into the room. "Seriously, Caleb, if that kid doesn't shut up, I'm gonna kill him. I haven't slept for three nights because of that crybaby."

The wails stop, but then the sniffles start. Which are actually worse than the wailing.

"Julio, give the kid a break," I say.

"You're too soft, Caleb. Gotta toughen these kids up."

"So they can be like you? No offense, man, but you'd scare a serial killer," I say.

One look at Julio and you know he's a tough guy. Tattoos all over his neck, back, and arms. Shaved head. When my mom comes for visits, she acts like his tattoos are contagious.

"So?" Julio says. "They gonna let you outta here?"

I sit on my bed. "Yeah. Tomorrow."

"Lucky sonofabitch. You goin' back to that small town with a funny name? Wha's it called again?"

"Paradise."

"So I'll be stuck here alone with crybaby while you're in Paradise? Ain't that a bitch." He gives the kid a wide-eyed stare. If I didn't know Julio better, I'd be afraid, too.

This sets the kid off again.

Julio chuckles, then says "Well, I'll give you the number to my cousin Rio in Chicago. If you need to hightail it out of Paradise, Rio will hook you up."

"Thanks, man," I say.

Julio shakes his head at the crying kid, says "Later, *amigo*," and leaves the open cell.

I tap the kid on his shoulder. He jerks away, scared.

"I'm not gonna hurt you," I tell him.

He turns to me. "That's what they all say. I heard about what goes on in jails." He scoots his butt towards the wall.

"Don't flatter yourself, kid. You're not my type. I like chicks."

"What about the guy with the tattoos?"

I fight the urge to laugh. "He's hetero, too. Dude, you're in a juvenile facility."

"He said he'll *kill* me."

"He says that because he likes you," I assure him. Julio has a sick sense of humor. "Now get off the bed, stop the crying, and go to group."

Group is group therapy. Where all the inmates sit around and discuss personal shit about their lives.

Tomorrow I'm getting the hell out of this place. No more group. No more cellmates. No more crappy food. No more cleaning dumpsters.

Tomorrow I'm going home.